THE LAST FREE RANGE

Also by James A. Ritchie

Kerrigan
The Payback
Over on the Lonesome Side

THE LAST FREE RANGE

James A. Ritchie

Walker and Company
New York

First published in the United States of America in 1995 by
Walker Publishing Company, Inc.

Published simultaneously in Canada by Thomas Allen & Son Canada,
Limited, Markham, Ontario

Library of Congress Cataloging-in-Publication Data
Ritchie, James A.
The last free range / James A. Ritchie.
p. cm.
ISBN 0-8027-4150-9
I. Title.
PS3568.I814L37   1995
813'.54—dc20   95-13051
CIP

Printed in the United States of America

2   4   6   8   10   9   7   5   3   1

*To Sandi Levy and Michael Rigg,
names that shall one day grace
the cover of many a fine novel.*

*And to Jackie Johnson, who edited
this novel while I was idling time
away in the intensive care unit.
Thanks, Jackie. You did a great job.*

THE WILD WIND

The Wild Wind blows toward freedom,
And fills the Heart's main sail,
If Only a man is brave enough,
To catch and hold its tail.

—Found in a Colorado bunkhouse, June 1886. Author unknown.

Author's Note

The above poem is the real theme behind *The Last Free Range*.

I'd like to think it was written by a dreaming cowboy who found the courage to grab the Wild Wind's tail and hold on until it carried him beyond the last strand of barbed wire.

If you know anything about this poem, have seen it in print before, or know the cowboy who wrote it, or if you simply have comments about *The Last Free Range*, please let me know. Address the letter to me at 91 Stonegate Drive, New Castle, IN, 47362.

THE LAST FREE
RANGE

CHAPTER 1

I WAS IN the bunkhouse, stripped to my longjohns, when Floyd Lowery came in to pay off the summer hands. I had my left foot in a pan of saltwater, soaking a cut on my heel that was threatening to fester, so I took the pay envelope and stuck it into a boot without bothering to count it.

Billy Martin was next to get a pay envelope, and that kind of surprised me. Billy was less than half my age, and a good hand. I'd expected the boss to keep him on.

"Sorry, Billy," Lowery said. "I put in a good word for you, but this is a small ranch and the boss said we got too many hands as it is."

"I'll find something," Billy muttered.

Lowery handed out three more envelopes, walked back to the door. "Don't know if it'll do you any good," he said, "but I hear the Rocking M is hiring. Might be a long ride for nothing. Try it if you want."

Lowery went on through the door. I swung my foot out of the saltwater, dried it, wrapped it with a cotton rag. Bud Shavers looked toward the door. "One thing about Floyd Lowery," he said. "Can't nobody say he ain't a compassionate son of a bitch."

Nobody argued the point. Billy was on the bunk across from me. He tore open his envelope and counted his wages.

"They sure don't throw any bonus money around," he said. "This is worked out to the last penny." He looked over at me. "What'll you do for the winter, Ben?"

"Ride down to the Rocking M, I reckon. It's that or the

1

grub line. Though it's in my mind to look for town work if the Rocking M don't pan out."

"I heard bad things about that outfit," Larry said. "Way I hear it, they hire a man as much for his fightin' as for his workin'."

I said nothing. Stretching out on my bunk, I pulled the thin blanket up over my shoulders, turned my head to the wall, and closed my eyes. After a time somebody blew out the lamp and I went to sleep.

Wakin' up in the morning ain't any harder than it ever was, but moving my body once I'm awake is. Seems like every joint I have stiffens up in the night. Still in my bunk, I stretched legs and arms, flexed my hands a bit, trying to chase away the stiffness before sitting up. If it hadn't been for a full bladder, I might not have made it up at all.

When I did sit up it still hurt right down my spine. I groaned. Johnny Stevens dangled his legs off his bunk and looked toward me. "How the hell old are you, anyway, Hawkins?"

"Too damned old," I said. "Why?"

"I mean it. How long you been a workin' cowhand?"

I had to think about it. "Since the war ended. What is that, near sixteen years?"

"That makes you what, forty?"

"I'll be forty-six next month. What are you getting at?"

"Nothing. Just thinkin', is all. I'll be twenty-five in a week. Guess I'm wondering what kind of a future I have."

"Don't go by me. Ain't many my age still pushing somebody else's cows around the range."

Billy had been lying awake on his bunk, listening to me and Johnny talk. Now he sat up, coughed, rubbed his head. "Didn't you ever want a ranch of your own?"

"Hell, every thick-between-the-ears cowboy I ever knew wanted his own spread. It takes more than wanting. There's still land for the taking here and there, but the day's long gone when a man could round up enough wild cattle to build a herd. I reckon I wanted a ranch, but I never could make it work."

"You must have made a lot of money in twenty years," Billy said. "What happened to it?"

I pulled on my pants. "Same damn thing that'll happen to yours. You ride into town with a month's wages, get drunk a couple of times, then when you get lonely enough and drunk enough to stand the smell, you buy a poke from an upstairs gal at the first cathouse you can find.

"If you have any money left afterward, you play poker and drink more whiskey. By Monday you start work broke. Now and again you manage to save enough for a new pair of boots or a good saddle, but not often.

"Money? Hell, if the boss didn't give his hands a fine bunkhouse to live in, and enough beans to keep their belt buckles from rubbing their backbones raw, every cowboy I ever knowed would be riding into town at night to beg for small change."

Billy Martin came from a family up Dallas way and hadn't grown up working cows like most of the men. He'd only been at it two years now, but he was eager and quick to learn. If he was being let go, then the boss was cutting hands to the rock bottom. But Billy was young, and he'd have an easier time finding winter work than most of us.

Me, I'd done without work before and would again. But I was too damned old to like it.

"If it's all right," Billy said, "I'd like to ride down to the Rocking M with you."

"Fine with me. What about you, Johnny?"

"Got nowheres else to go. I'll tag along."

There's no point in hanging around a place once you get your last wages, so after a greasy breakfast of salt pork and biscuits, we saddled our horses and rode southwest, heading toward Pecos River territory.

It was near the end of fall, chilly but not yet cold, and good weather for riding. The Rocking M was better than a hundred miles west and fifty miles south, and it made me wonder how Floyd Lowery knew they were hiring.

Not that word about ranches don't get around. And most everybody knew something or another about the Rocking M. Neal Pierce started the ranch right after the war, and now it had grown enough to give Pierce a reputation.

After leaving the ranch, we stopped off and picked up a few supplies—beans, salt pork, and coffee, mostly. That night I did the cooking, and somehow or other Billy and Johnny both got it down without much complaining.

We rode along easy like, and about noon the next day we made camp next to a trickle of water big enough to keep the horses happy and small enough to step across without getting our boots wet.

Billy made the coffee, and while drinking it we talked. Talk jumps from one subject to another over a campfire, and we discussed such things as the best ranch we'd worked on, the best wrecks we'd had or seen, the best horse we'd owned, and everything else that comes from being a workin' cowhand.

And as it will, talk turned to outlaws and gunfighters and those who chase them. West Texas had plenty of outlaws, too damn many gunfighters, and not nearly enough lawmen to go around.

When you get to talking about such things, sooner or later the talk works around in a circle and ends with the gun you're wearing or, more likely, carrying in your saddlebags. Most young cowhands practice a fast draw and spend time shooting at tin cans or snakes and such, but most give it up the first time they come close to putting a bullet through their own foot.

Me, I'd never got started. I hunted and such, growing up, but never with a short gun. Fact is, the first time I ever fired one was during the war. I'd used one since, but not often, and never when drawing fast was a matter of concern.

Billy was at the age where he still looked up to gunfighters, and I guess maybe Johnny was too. So after a time they started bragging about their skill, and pretty soon they were hunting up targets. There wasn't much about, but they picked up a bunch of fist-sized rocks from that trickle of water.

Billy lined the rocks up on the ground, placing them two feet apart and twenty yards or so from camp. Johnny showed off his skill first, drawing fast and firing five times. His first two shots missed by a foot, the third hit a rock dead center, the fourth missed again, and the fifth nicked a rock and screamed off into the sky.

Billy tried his hand next. He drew about as fast as Johnny had, but hit only one rock. He didn't miss the others by more than a foot or so, hitting low each time.

While reloading their Colts, they both looked at me. "Get up here and show us what you can do," Johnny said.

I shook my head. "Next to me, you two are Wild Bill Hickok and Jim Courtright. Nope, I reckon I'll just sit here and drink my coffee."

"Ah, come on," Billy said. "Ain't no harm in tryin'."

"Oh, let him alone," Johnny said. "A man gets to be as old as Ben, why, he needs his rest. Can't expect him to compete with young bucks like us."

Johnny was smiling, and I had to smile right back. I drained the cup in my hand and stood up. "All right, Wild Bill, I'll try. You may have to help me, though. Old as I am, it might be I can't hang on to my Colt."

My Colt and holster were wrapped in a cotton cloth and stuck down in a saddlebag. I dug it out, stripped off my jacket, and belted the holster around my waist. I faced the rocks, but not wanting to risk shooting either us or the horses, I didn't even think about drawing fast.

Lifting the Colt from the holster, I lined it up with the

first rock, thumbing back the hammer as it came up. Only when the sights were settled did I squeeze the trigger. The Colt bucked in my hand and the first rock jumped three feet into the air.

Spacing my shots about three seconds apart, I hit three out of five rocks, missing the last two by four or five inches.

"That's pretty good shooting," Johnny said. "But a man could die of old age before you put a bullet in him."

I shrugged, took the time to reload the Colt before speaking. "Always figured it was better to hit slow than to miss fast," I said. "Some might argue the point, but it's got me this far."

We still had wages burning a hole in our pockets, so on the fourth day we stopped off in Stillwater, thinking to get out of the weather for a time and shed as much of our money as the small saloon there could handle.

A man makes two kinds of friends: those he has to be with because of work or whatever, and those he chooses to ride with. The three of us were riding together by choice, and that made us friends of the best sort: it made us partners.

On the second day in town we bought a bottle and were sitting at a table drinking when half a dozen men came in. Already better than half drunk, they ordered more whiskey and began trying to bait one of us into a fight.

One of them, a big, butt-ugly man of thirty or so, decided to pick on me. He called me grandpa a couple of times, said he didn't think an old fart like me could still sit a horse. I threw a drink down my throat and stood up. "How much do you weigh?" I asked.

His face opened a little in surprise. "Huh, how the hell would I know? What difference does it make?"

" 'Cause I hear horse manure is going for a dollar a ton, and I wondered if you were worth hauling off."

Half a dozen men laughed. Then he hit me. I saw his

fist coming, but not in time. It caught me on the cheek and knocked me back against the table. I shook my head and charged back in. Folks formed a circle, giving us room, and for five minutes we went at it.

I could dimly hear men shouting for me to stretch him out, and others yelling even louder for him to kick me back to Dallas. The shouts seemed a long way off, almost covered by the rasping of my lungs. He was winning, or it felt like he was, but the truth is we were both too drunk to really do much harm.

Then I landed a good right hand on the bridge of his nose. I've been hit there, and it hurts. He grabbed his nose and staggered back. It was a punch that hurt some, but did him no real harm. He reached over to a table and picked up a glass of whiskey a fellow had left sitting, drank it with a swallow, then closed his hands into fists.

The room was already spinning a bit, but I raised my own fists and stepped unsteadily toward him. But before I could take a step something exploded on the side of my head and everything went black.

When my eyes opened again I tried to move. It hurt, so I stayed still and tried to squint the blur out of my vision. After a time it worked. Then I saw bars and knew I was in jail. I groaned, tried to sit up. Again, it took some time, but I made it.

" 'Bout time you woke up," somebody said. "I was beginning to think the marshal hit you too hard."

Looking toward the voice, I saw the man I'd been fighting with. He was in the next cell, holding a cup of coffee. The side of his face toward me had a black eye, and his nose seemed out of kilter. "The marshal?"

He nodded. "Un-huh. I heard he was out to the Johnsons', or I'd never've picked a fight. Marshal Kinser takes fighting unkindly. He laid you out with the barrel of his Colt."

The side of my head throbbed with pain, most of it coming from just behind the ear. I also had a hangover, and my lips felt twice as big as they should've been. On top of that, my spine hurt from top to bottom. I didn't seem to be hurt in any serious way, but I felt like I'd been spurred through close cactus and run into a wide tree.

"My name's Jess Baker," the man said. "What do they call you?"

I stood up, stretched my back, groaned. "Hawkins. Ben Hawkins. Where'd you get the java?"

"From the marshal. Hold on."

He stood up, moved to the front of his cell, yelled through the bars. A minute later a door opened and a man stuck his head in. "What is it?"

"That fella you clouted is awake. I reckon he could use some coffee, and I wouldn't turn down another cup myself."

The head disappeared, came back a minute later. This time the man came all the way in. He was a tall, almost skinny man with black hair and a big mustache. A badge was pinned to his vest. He carried a coffeepot in one hand and a tin cup in the other. He refilled Jess's cup, handed me the cup he held, and filled it to the brim.

"Thanks," I said. "Why'd you hit me, anyway?"

"Nothing personal," he said. "I found the best way to stop a fight without argument is to lay somebody out. You was closest. Didn't think I hit you that hard. You all right?"

"I'll live. Reckon the whiskey put me out as much as you did."

"That was my thinking. None of my business, but ain't you a little long in the tooth to be brawling in a bar with with a man half your age?"

"I reckon he's more than half my age, but I won't argue the point."

"Where you headed?"

"Heard the Rocking M was hiring. I could sure use winter work." The coffee was hot and felt almost as good as it tasted. "When can I get out of here?"

"I'm supposed to hold you twenty-four hours, but you don't look like you'll be fighting again anytime soon. You want breakfast first?"

"Breakfast? You mean I been in here all night?"

"That's a fact. What about the breakfast?"

My stomach was rolling. "Nope. But you can top off this coffee."

He refilled the inch of coffee I'd drunk. Then he walked back into his office and returned with the key to the cell. He opened the door. "You can stay until you finish your coffee," he said. "What about you, Jess? You want food?"

"Why not?"

"I'll have it brought over. Biscuits and gravy do you?"

"Long as it's hot."

Marshal Kinser left again. I sat down on the cot, sipped the coffee, rubbed my head, felt for tobacco. I found papers, but no sack. Jess came out of his cell and into mine, tossed me tobacco. I rolled a smoke, struck a lucifer, lit the cigarette, inhaled. "Thanks. Why'd you pick a fight last night, if you don't mind my asking?"

"Since when does a man need a reason? I get to drinkin' and then I get to fightin'. What else is there to do on a Saturday night?"

"I can think of a thing or two. And why me?"

Jess rolled a smoke of his own. "Hell, I done whupped everbody I know. Them fellas with you was younger, but you looked tougher. Figured you might put up a fight." He touched his nose gently and winced. "You didn't let me down."

"I think you were winning."

"Maybe. But the truth is, I was too drunk last night to know or care."

We talked until a plump, middle-aged lady brought in a tray of food. Jess dug into it while I finished my coffee.

Then I eased my hat onto my head and left the cell, going through the door and into the office.

Marshal Kinser looked up from his desk. "Couple of boys came looking for you earlier," he said. "You were still sleeping, so I told 'em to try later. They haven't been back."

"I'll find 'em. Thanks."

"You stay outa trouble. I'd hate to abuse my Colt by hitting you twice in twenty-four hours."

"Yes, sir. Reckon we'll be gone before long."

Stepping out onto the boardwalk, I sucked in the air, hoping it would ease the ache behind my eyes. It didn't. The day was cool, but the sun was bright, so I pulled my hat down low and went looking for Billy and Johnny. I found them in the saloon.

"I'll be danged," Billy said, "look who decided to come home."

Johnny grinned. "Damn, Hawkins, you look like hell warmed over. Pull up a chair and have a beer."

"Ain't no fool like an old fool," I said.

Pulling up a chair, I had two beers. Then, with my head still pounding, we picked up our horses and rode on toward the Rocking M.

CHAPTER 2

NOW, THAT COUNTRY down along the Pecos don't generally get anything like the blizzards that sometimes sweep across the high plains, but it gets chilly enough. From time to time it drops below freezing, and the snow comes down hard. But mostly the winters are just damned chilly, and wet enough to make the chill go all the way through a man.

I guess how cold you call it depends on what you're used to, but I'm a cold-blooded man by nature. I like my weather hot, else it seems my bones turn to peanut brittle.

Another month and it would be full winter, and like I say, there was just no telling how cold it might get. The nights were already cold enough to make a man wish he had a bigger fire and an extra blanket, but the days were pleasant, just cool enough to make a man sit in the sun rather than in the shade.

Near as I could tell, there wasn't no boundary of any kind marking the beginning of the Rocking M range, but there came a time when three men rode up to us and asked our business. All three men were loaded for bear.

The biggest man, the one who did most of the talking, wore a Colt, which was normal enough, but he had a second tucked into his waistband. He also carried a rifle, and a double-barreled shotgun hung from his saddle, supported by a leather thong.

Both of the other men were similarly armed, and all three men had old boot tops fastened to their saddles. A piece of leather was fastened across the bottom, closing it off so it would hold things. These boot tops were filled with cartridges. It was a trick used by rustlers and others who

11

figured to need ammunition in a hurry, and spelled out plain that the three men weren't cowhands.

Anyhow, those three rode up in front of us an' we stopped to see what they wanted.

"My name's Hank Collins," the big man said. "Mind tellin' me where you're headed?"

"Can't see where it's any of your business," I said, "but we heard the Rocking M was hiring. Figured to ride over and see."

"It's our business," Collins said. "We work for the Rocking M."

"You do the hiring?"

"No, but that's got nothing to—"

"Then it seems to me it ain't your business, after all. You just tell us how to find the foreman, an' we'll be on our way."

It was plain Collins didn't like what I'd said and probably didn't like me. I paid him no nevermind. One of the others spoke up then. He was a smaller man, but his voice was the kind you don't ignore.

"Two miles straight down the road. Ask for a fellow named Foster Smith. Tell him Brice Campbell sent you."

"Obliged."

Hank Collins's face flushed a little and he opened his mouth to say something. He never had a chance. Brice Campbell glanced his way. "Shut up, Hank."

Hank shut up so fast you could hear his teeth click together, and we went on down the road. We'd ridden maybe two hundred yards when Johnny looked over at me. "Never thought I'd meet a man like Brice Campbell around here."

"You know Campbell?"

Johnny's jaw dropped wide open. "Hell, man, you mean you never heard of Brice Campbell?"

I shrugged. "Not that I recall."

Johnny shook his head. "You beat all, Hawkins. Brice

Campbell is a range detective, and they say he's the best hand with a gun you ever saw. The big ranchers hire him to clean out rustlers and the like.

"They say he's killed fifteen men. Hell, you can't sit down to a campfire or go into a saloon without somebody bringing up his name."

"Guess I just never paid attention."

The Rocking M ranch house was tucked away behind a hill, and we stopped to look it over. Three men were doing their best to break a few horses in a big corral out behind a barn, and I counted a dozen saddled horses in front of the ranch house.

A group of men, maybe six or eight, mingled in front of the house, and on the porch I could see a couple of others.

"What do you suppose that's all about?" Billy asked.

"We won't find out sitting here," I said. "Let's go see about a job."

We rode into the ranch yard and on up to the porch. Folks turned to watch us, and the men on the porch stopped talking. I looked at the two men standing there. One was my age, or a bit older, and was wearing a white shirt, brown pants, and a matching brown vest. He also wore a short-barreled Colt with grips carved from an antler.

The second man was younger, and a bit shorter. His hair was black, and his mustache was neatly trimmed. The older man spoke. "Can I help you boys?"

"Looking for work," Billy said. "Fellow told us you were hiring."

"We ran into Brice Campbell down the road a piece," Johnny added. "He said to tell you he sent us on in."

"That do make a difference," the older man said. "My name is Neal Pierce, and I own the Rocking M. This man here is Foster Smith. He does the hiring and firing."

Foster Smith took half a step forward and hooked his thumbs in his gunbelt. "We could use a couple more good men," he said, "but we need men who can handle a gun as well as they can cattle. Any of you fit that bill?"

"Mister," I said, "I'm looking to handle cattle, but it sounds like you might be expecting trouble. Trouble comes to the brand I'm workin' for, and I'll take a hand. But I ain't one to go looking for it."

"You had so many offers you can afford to be choosy?"

"No, sir, and I don't look forward to riding the grub line all winter. Just want to know where I stand, is all."

"That's a fair question, so I'll answer it. There's trouble brewing, and I'll not lie about it. Mr. Pierce here built this ranch, and he paid for it a hundred times over with sweat and the blood of good men.

"Other folks are trying to move in, and they figure to cut the range up. Some are stringing barbed wire. You can see where that leaves us."

"Yes, sir. It leaves you needin' to prove the land is yours, and to do that, you have to hold it."

Neal Pierce stepped right to the edge of the porch. "I'll hold my land," he said. "Without guns, if possible, but I won't let anyone cut off the water supply with wire. If you hire on here, I'll expect you to do as you're told, and if that means cutting wire and chasing out nesters, then by God, you'll do it."

I felt old. Old and tired. "No, sir, I reckon not. Guess I'll keep looking. I've had enough trouble to do me."

Foster turned his attention to Billy and Johnny. "What about you two?"

"I can use a gun," Johnny said. "Don't know as I want to, but I can."

"It pays fifty a month and found," Foster said. "It'll be more if shooting starts."

Johnny turned to me. "What do you think, Hawkins?"

"It's your call, Johnny. It sounds like a range war coming, but it might straighten itself out. If not, you'll likely have to use your Colt on men. But that's your call, too."

Johnny turned back to Foster. "Riding the grub line don't suit me," he said. "You've hired yourself a man."

Foster looked at Billy. "You're a little young, but I won't hold that against you. Can you handle a Colt?"

"Well enough, but I guess I'll ride along with Ben and see what turns up."

"Fair enough. Good luck to you both."

"Doggone it," Johnny said. "I hate to break up the threesome."

"Don't worry about it, Johnny. "We'll likely be around come spring. It might work out that we'll ride together again."

We shook hands, then I turned back to Foster Smith. "What's the closest town?" I asked.

"Place called Comanche Creek. Take the road four miles west and you can't miss it. Not much of a place, but they have a saloon."

"Most every town does."

Billy and me rode out, but we hadn't made more than a mile when I could tell Billy had an itch in his saddle.

"Wishing you'd stayed on back there?"

"No, Ben, I ain't. If you say there's trouble coming, then I guess you been around long enough to know. But I ain't looking forward to riding the grub line, neither."

"Can't say I don't feel the same. That's why I want a look about town. Might be some kind of work a man can do there."

"In town! What kind of work can a man do in a town?"

"Hell, I don't know. That's why I'm going in. I've done a bit of smithy work. Got to be something that needs doing."

A mile passed in silence, though the way Billy kept looking at me, I knew he had something on his mind. After a time I asked what it was.

"Just wondering about you, Ben. You seemed real set on avoiding trouble, but I seem to recall you once saying you'd been in the war. That right?"

"I was. Guess maybe that's why I've not gone looking for trouble since. I saw a lot of men die, Billy, and God only knows how many I killed. It kind of filled me up on trouble."

"You ain't had no trouble since the war?"

"I didn't say that. I went up the Chisholm Trail near a dozen times. But I was working and the trouble came to me. Wasn't no way around it."

We rode on to Comanche Creek, and like Foster said, it wasn't much of a town. It had a saloon, a blacksmith shop and livery, a mercantile, a small bank, a barbershop, and maybe two hundred people to keep them all afloat. A good part of the time the livery and the blacksmith shop are one and the same in a small town, and that's how it was at Comanche Creek. So when we settled our horses, I had a chance to ask about work at the same time.

The blacksmith was a man a bit above medium height and built like a bull. It was a fine, cool day, but his face and bare arms glistened with sweat from working over the forge and swinging a heavy hammer. His red hair and beard were streaked with gray, and I figured him to be about my age. When I asked about work, he straightened up and wiped the sweat on his forehead.

"I could use a man," he said. "If you know what you're doing. What I don't need is somebody who wants to learn. You don't already know how to mend a wheel or shape a shoe, you'd best look elsewhere."

"I can do either. Been a few years, but I can do most anything around a smithy."

"Where'd you learn?"

"My pa taught me. He owned a smithy the whole time I was growing up."

He nodded. "My name is Charlie Heinlin. Folks mostly call me Red. I'll give you a try, if you don't mind part-time work. It'll be three days a week to begin with.

"I'd like to offer you more, but things are a little slow.

Come Friday and Saturday I can use help, and on Sundays I like to take a buggy and go see my daughter. I can give you ten bits a day and a room to sleep in."

"Sounds good. My name is Ben Hawkins."

"All right, Ben. You be here along about dark and I'll show you where to sleep. Tomorrow morning we'll see how well your pa taught you."

"That's fine. Anyplace about to get a bite of food?"

"Just the saloon. Up till a week ago an old lady named Mabel Radford ran an eatery, but she up and died on us. Now it's just the saloon."

I didn't have to ask how the food was. I'd eaten saloon food in four states and one territory, and there wasn't a penny's difference in the lot. Storing most of our gear in a small toolroom at the smithy, we strolled over to the saloon and went inside. It wasn't much past noon and only a few souls were there, more of them drinking than eating.

I still had eleven dollars left from my wages, and Billy claimed to have a bit more, and that would get us by for a time even without a job if we were careful. But with a part-time job at the smithy, I didn't have to worry about being too careful, so after eating a bowl of stew, I ordered a second beer and sat in on a poker game just starting up at a corner table.

Billy thought about sitting in, but decided against it since he hadn't found work. But he did buy himself another beer and sat down close enough to watch the game. The game was five-card draw and we played for low stakes, two bits being the limit. A game like that ain't much, but a man can still lose more than you'd think. So I played cautiously, waiting to bet until I had a hand. Then, when the other men got to thinking they knew me, I bluffed a hand and dragged in three dollars.

After three hours I was nearly seven dollars ahead and starting to have second thoughts about taking a job bending iron over a hot forge. Then Hank Collins came into the saloon. Our eyes met. He didn't nod. Ten minutes later he came to the table and sat down to join the game.

Hank Collins had been riding with Brice Campbell, and that might mean he was good with a gun, but I had no way of telling for sure. But after an hour I did know one thing about Collins—he was a lousy poker player. He raised and tried to bluff every two or three hands, and when he did catch good cards he gave himself away and we all dropped out. At the end of two hours he was twelve dollars down, most of it lost to me.

Hank Collins had begun the game laughing, joking, talking almost constantly. But the more he lost, the quieter he got. And then the quiet turned to mumbling. I'd seen men like him before and figured to quit before he started trouble. But I played one hand too many.

It was my deal, and when I looked at my cards I found three aces looking back. I raised and Hank Collins raised again. I raised him back and he called. He took one card and I took two.

I caught a pair of deuces that gave me a full house, but Collins stayed through three raises before calling. When I laid down the ace full he swore and threw his cards.

Collins came out of his chair and stood straight up, his hand just below the butt of his Colt. "You can't be doing that honest," he said. "I say you're a cheat! A dirty, bottom-dealing cheat!"

You never heard a saloon go quiet so fast in your life.

CHAPTER 3

LOOKING AT THE other men around the table, I spoke. "Anybody else feel that way?"

They looked at each other. "No," one of them said. "It was a fair deal."

"I say it was a crooked deal," Collins said. "And I say you're a cheat."

Slowly standing up, I spoke easy. "Just let it drop. I don't want no trouble."

"Trouble's already here. You're wearin' a Colt. Use it."

"Don't be a damned fool, Collins. It ain't worth killing a man over a few dollars."

"It's worth it to me. You going to draw, or admit you was cheating?"

I swore. The whole thing made me mad, and I swore long and loud. Then I started around the table. I don't know if it was the anger in my voice, the look on my face, or just the surprise of me coming around at him, but Collins started backing away.

Then I was around the table. "What are you doin'?" he asked. "Draw, damn you."

I kept coming and he kept backing away. Then his rear hit a table and he staggered a little. He tried to draw then, but I was right on top of him. When his hand touched his Colt I hit him. My fist caught him on the mouth and snapped his head back. He fumbled with the Colt and it fell to the floor. Another pistol was stuck behind his waistband, but I paid it no mind.

I hit him twice more, and on the second blow I felt a tooth snap under my knuckle. Collins went down. Bend-

19

ing, I snatched the pistol from behind his belt and skidded it away across the floor.

Collins was spitting blood, and he was stunned. But he roared and came to his feet. Waiting until he was up, I ducked under a wide right and hit him in the belly. He was soft there, and the air went out of him with a whoosh. He backed up, gasping for air that wouldn't come.

Slamming him against the wall, I hit him three more times in the belly, then stepped away. He fell to the floor, trying to retch up everything he'd eaten all day long.

I was breathing hard, and I was shaking. Shaking from anger, and from the suddenness of the fight. Everyone in the saloon was looking at me, and only when I sat back down at the table and took a long drink of beer did they begin to look away, going back to their own business.

My hand hurt and I looked at it. The first knuckle on my right hand was swollen a little, and the second knuckle was split enough for a big drop of blood to appear through the skin. But when I worked my hand it moved all right and I didn't think anything was broken.

Billy dropped into a chair next to me. "For a man who claims not to like fighting," he said, "you sure seem to get into a lot of 'em."

"Always been the way with me for some reason."

A chair scraped and somebody sat down at the table across from me. Looking up, I saw it was Brice Campbell. He was smiling. "Would've been easier just to shoot him," Campbell said.

"Maybe."

"I figured you for a fighting man," he said, "but Foster said you spoke down about yourself. That right?"

I shrugged. "Just said I'd had enough trouble. And that's a fact. Didn't say I couldn't handle it if it came my way."

"Hell, nothing wrong with that, man. I'd just as soon avoid it myself, truth be known."

"That's a funny thing for a hired gun to say."

"Is it? Hell, maybe you're right. But it's true. I do what has to be done, but given my druthers, I'd do it peaceful every time. Only, some folks won't listen to reason."

"And when that happens?"

"Like I said, then I do what has to be done. That don't mean I have to like it. . . . Seems we might have something in common, Hawkins. I told the boss he should've talked you into staying. How are you with a short gun?"

"Slow and steady. I hit where I aim if I got enough time, but I ain't nothin' on the draw."

"Fast don't always mean much. If it comes to trouble, half that bunch he hired'll cut and run at the first shot. No, sir, it's nerve that counts, and you got nerve a-plenty."

"Because of Collins? That wasn't nerve. He just made me mad, was all. If I'd had any sense I'd have turned around and walked out."

"Bet you were in the war."

"Most men my age were."

"Bet you saw a lot of action, too."

"A bit."

"Damn it . . . what was your given name?"

"Ben."

"Ben, yeah. Well, damn it, Ben, you ain't an easy man to get to know."

"Guess I don't talk much about myself."

Campbell yelled for the bartender to bring over three whiskeys with beer chasers. Only when they were at the table did he speak again. He lifted his glass of whiskey. "Here's to fast horses an' faster women," he said.

I grinned. Lifting my glass, I drank with him, chased the whiskey with a swallow of beer.

"That job offer is still open," he said. "We could use a good man like you." He looked at Billy. "That goes for you too."

"Thanks," I said, "but I already got a job working at the smithy."

"All right if I keep you in mind?" Billy asked. "I'd like to look around for a day or two."

"Sure thing. If nothing else turns up, ride out to the ranch and we'll put you to work."

Campbell finished his beer and stood up. "You're a strange man, Hawkins. Be damned if you ain't. Well, I'll see you around."

He walked away and I sat there for a spell, taking my time with the beer in my hand. A little before dark we walked back over to see Red Heinlin's smithy. He was just finishing up for the day when we walked into the shop.

"You been drinkin'?" he asked me.

"Yes, sir. Been fightin' too."

He shook his head. "Well, I'll tell you straight out," he said. "I take a drink or two myself, and I won't hold that agin you. But don't drink while you're working, and don't come in so hung over you can't work."

"I never do."

"Then we'll get along. Grab your things and I'll show you where to hang your hat."

"You think there'll be room for Billy? He's looking for work, but it might take some time."

"Up to you, I guess. Come on."

I expected a room somewhere at the back of the livery, but Red led us to a small house fifty yards behind the livery. We didn't go in, but around to the far side of the house. A small, neatly painted building sat there, and Red opened the door. "Used to be my shop," he said. "Only after a time I outgrew it, so I turned it into what you see here."

What I saw was a clean, tight, two-room shack. The larger room held a cookstove, a table with three chairs, and an old bureau. There was also a cabinet and a washbasin against the far wall. The room in back was smaller, but had a decent-sized bed and a closet big enough to hold clothing and a bit of gear.

Some mightn't call it much, but it was better than any bunkhouse I'd ever hung my hat in.

"Try to keep it clean," Red told me, "or the missus will hang me up to dry."

"Yes, sir. We'll watch ourselves. And speaking of clean, I was wonderin' about a bath? Does the barbershop have a tub or the like?"

"Used to, but Hank Barton got tired of drunks staggering in wanting a bath, so he sold it off for junk. The saloon has a couple of barrels in a shack out back where a man can soak himself, though."

"Got any idea what it costs?"

"Depends what else you want along with gettin' clean."

I knew what he meant. The bath might cost four bits, throw in a bottle and that's another dollar. Take one of the upstairs girls out with you and there goes three or four or five more dollars. Comanche Creek might have been a small town, but they kept right up with the big cities in some ways.

Having seen where he was going to sleep, Billy stowed his gear and decided to head back to the saloon for a time. Wanting a bath, I walked along with him. Turned out there was three barrels set up in a building out behind the saloon, blankets hung to separate them. Several buckets sat next to a pump, and there was a woodstove to heat the water if you didn't want a cold bath.

I was alone when I went into the bathhouse, but by the time I had my water hot and was soaking in a barrel, two cowboys came in, each with a bottle in one hand and a girl under his arm. Being alone, I hadn't bothered to pull the blanket over so as to block off view from the other barrels, and they were too drunk to care.

The cowboys stripped down and climbed into the barrels and the girls poured buckets of hot water over them.

I soaked for a while, accepted a drink from one of the cowboys, then dressed and went back to my room. Billy drifted in a bit after midnight and crawled into bed alongside me.

Come morning I started work with Red Heinlin. It took an hour or so to get my touch back, but then I found the rhythm of the hammer. Knowing how to tell the glowing metal was ready to come out of the forge just by looking at it soon came back to me.

I always liked doing smithy work. There's a pleasure in the sweat and the heat and the pull of the muscles, and I'd thought about doing it for a living a time or two, but it seemed like something always got in the way.

First the war came along, and then it was punching cattle. The war they could keep, but I liked sitting astride a good cutting horse, and I liked being out on the range with no roof except for the hat on my head.

But, hell, I was getting old. My spine felt like dry wood of a morning, and my hands and knees ached considerable from the time I woke up until noon. Likely I was getting a case of rheumatism. Couldn't complain if I was. You wreck enough wild horses, and coming through with no more than a little pain of a morning is a cheap price. But it wasn't only the horses.

Throw in pushing cows through cold streams and riding herd through fall rains, winter snows, and anything else the good Lord thought of to hinder a cowhand, and I couldn't complain at all.

Red Heinlin seemed pleased enough with my work, and it suited me fine. I wasn't going to get rich from it, nor even be able to put much back toward spring, but I didn't care. There was money enough for food, a few beers, and a poker game now and again, so I was content with my lot.

Billy stayed with me for a week, then found work of his own. A woman named Beth Alison came into town, looking to hire hands for the winter; Billy snapped up the offer.

"Never thought I'd work for a woman," he said, "but this one is prettier than a west Texas sunset. You should ride out and meet her, Ben."

I promised I would one day, and Billy packed his gear and went along to her ranch.

From time to time he came back into town and we had a beer together. Billy said Beth Alison had put him in a line shack with another fellow, and all they had to do all winter long was ride the fence and patch any breaks or cuts.

Mrs. Alison, it seemed, had spent all summer stringing barbed wire, and while the Rocking M had made noise, there'd been no trouble. Beth didn't believe there would be.

Johnny Stevens also came in a couple of times, but he told a different story from Billy. He said Neal Pierce was getting madder by the day, and Johnny expected the shooting to start anytime. Johnny was right.

Just a week later, some cowhands from Mrs. Alison's ranch and half a dozen from the Rocking M came to town at the same time. Brice Campbell and Hank Collins were among the Rocking M riders.

I came out of the shadows where the forge sat and walked over to the anvil. I was holding a hot piece of metal in tongs, fixing to hammer it into a hinge for a wagon box, when I looked over toward the saloon and saw the Rocking M riders tying up. I also saw the Reverse Box E horses already there. I'd learned from Billy that Beth Alison's brand was the Reverse Box E, though she didn't call her ranch that.

With only one saloon for miles around, riders from the Rocking M and riders from the Reverse Box E were often in the same room together, though they tended to stay to their own corner, so I thought nothing about it. Then I heard the shots. Two quick shots from a Colt, a space of five seconds, then a third shot.

Most folks got off the streets quick, ducking into the first door they passed. A few others, too curious or foolish for their own good, started running toward the saloon. I stayed where I was as men rushed out of the saloon, guns in hand. They jumped into the saddles of the Rocking M horses and rode out of town. Only then did I put aside my work and walk over to the saloon, and only because I knew Billy was in there.

Billy had a bullet hole in his sleeve, but the bullet hadn't touched his skin. One other Reverse Box E rider wasn't so lucky.

He was dead, two bullets in his chest. The only shot he'd got off went wild, and it was his bullet that almost hit Billy. There was a doctor in Comanche Creek, and he came running, but all he could do was confirm what we already knew. The man was dead.

"His name was Chance Evans," Billy said. "He was good hand with cattle."

"I hope somebody says as much about me when my time comes," I said. "What started the trouble, Billy?"

"Brice Campbell came in with the other riders. Said Pierce had reached his limit. He wasn't looking for trouble, Campbell said, but he couldn't let another strand of barbed wire go up.

"I told him it was Beth Alison he should be talking to. He said he would, and I thought that ended it. Then Evans told Campbell the Reverse Box E would string all the wire it wanted, and there wasn't a thing Pierce could do about it.

" 'If Mr. Pierce tells us to stop more wire from going up,' Campbell said, 'we'll stop it.'

"Evans wouldn't let it drop, Ben. He told Campbell to go to hell, and then he drew. I swear to God, Ben, I never saw Campbell's hand move. Quick? Lord God almighty, Ben. You wouldn't believe it!"

"Maybe the trouble will stop here."

"It's just starting, Ben. Evans was a favorite of Beth's, but that aside, she ain't about to stop putting up wire."

"You were lucky, Billy. This time it was one against one. Next time it might be an all-out fight. Might be you should quit Beth Alison. There's other jobs."

"Ben, I was scared in there. I never saw a man killed, and my heart was beating like mad. And Lord, my hands were shaking so bad I couldn't have hit anything with a Colt."

"Hell, Billy, anybody'd be scared."

"No, I mean I was really scared, Ben. I felt like my gut was gonna let loose. Thought sure I'd mess myself. That's how scared I was. But I can't quit. I took the job, and I'll ride for the brand.

"Am I wrong, Ben? Am I wrong to feel that way?"

"I don't think so. But it looks like you and Johnny are going to be on opposite sides."

"Hell, he wouldn't shoot at me, nor me at him."

"He wouldn't like to, but when the bullets start flying you can't always pick out your friends."

"What about being scared, Ben? I'm ashamed of that more than anything."

"No need to be. I been that scared myself. Sometimes you can't do nothing but be scared."

"I guess."

"But you're gonna stick it out?"

"I couldn't face myself otherwise."

Billy was his own man, and it wasn't my place to say can or can't, should or shouldn't. Some things a man has to do, and for Billy, this was one of them. And I knew how he felt. When the war broke out I ran to join. Come the first battle, with guns hammering and men dying hard and bloody, I was scared, too.

Not just scared. Terrified. The thought of running went through my mind, and if it hadn't been for a burly sergeant standing close by, I might have taken off. But I stayed, and it made a difference.

From time to time fear rose up again, but never like that first battle.

Billy's first battle came without him needing to kill or be killed, and he was lucky. Now he had to face his fear, or he'd always wonder if he was a coward. Foolish? Maybe. But that's how he felt, and I understood it.

I just hoped he didn't get killed on his way to finding out how brave a man he really was.

CHAPTER 4

TWO WEEKS OF relative calm followed the shooting in the saloon, but it was an unnatural calm, the kind you feel out on the range just before a thunderstorm hits. Having only one saloon in Comanche Creek complicated things a bit as well. Riders for both the Rocking M and the Reverse Box E liked to have a drink now and again, but after the shooting they went out of their way to avoid each other.

Neal Pierce had four times the number of men as the Reverse Box E, and most of these had been hired for their guns. It meant they came and went pretty much as they pleased, near taking over the saloon.

Billy was busy stringing wire, but he came into town twice over those two weeks. Each time he gave me money and I bought several bottles for him and his friends. Billy would load the bottles into his saddlebags and ride out to the ranch, so drinking wasn't a problem. Women were another matter.

The saloon had five girls ready and willing to sell a man a poke, and the Rocking M riders took full advantage. I reckon the Reverse Box E boys wanted a woman as much as anybody, but there wasn't a day when the saloon didn't have at least a few Rocking M riders occupying bar space.

I put in my three days a week working for Red, and tried my best to keep my views to myself. Two weeks of sleeping on a good bed and doing hard work had done wonders for my back and hands. They were still stiff and hurt a bit when I first woke up, but the pain faded within an hour or so.

There's a lot of heavy lifting to be done around a smithy,

and most of the work demands swinging a heavy hammer for hours on end. For the first weeks every muscle I had was sore, but that faded along with the pain in my spine, and after two full weeks I felt like a kid again.

I'd been meaning to ride out and meet Beth Alison as I'd promised Billy, but she beat me to it. It was a chilly Sunday afternoon, and Red was out of town visiting his daughter and her family. I was looking around, wondering whether to shoe a cussed mare or to finish repairing a wagon tongue.

The wagon tongue looked the easier of the two, and I set about taking the old tongue off the wagon. I hadn't been at it five minutes when a wagon rolled up in front, flanked by half a dozen riders. One of them was Billy.

A small man with a grizzled gray beard drove the wagon, and next to him sat the kind of woman fit to turn any man's head. Curly black hair hung well below her shoulders, and her face was a fine thing to see. She wore pants that fit better on her than they would've on any man, and a heavy jacket that hung open in spite of the cold breeze. The open jacket revealed a blue blouse and a figure that made me draw in a deep breath.

Billy dropped off his horse and gave the woman a hand down from the wagon. They both walked up to me. Billy introduced us, and Beth smiled. "Pleased to meet you, ma'am," I said.

"Billy has told me all about you," she said. "He tells me I should hire you."

"I've been through that, ma'am. I like it fine right here."

"Isn't there something I can do to change your mind?"

A woman with Beth's kind of looks shouldn't ask a man a question like that. "No, ma'am. I can't think of a thing you could say."

"How much are you paid here?"

"Enough to get by, I reckon."

"I mean it, how much? A dollar a day?"

"A bit more."

"Don't let him fool you, Miss Alison," Billy said. "Ben makes a dollar and two bits a day, but he don't work more'n three days a week."

"So in a good month you might earn fifteen dollars? That isn't very much money."

"It's enough."

"Is it? I'll give you seventy-five a month to ride for me."

The wind kicked up dust, whipped it through the open door of the smithy. Working kept me warm, but standing there talking to Beth Alison cooled me off fast. "No, ma'am. That's a good bit of money, but not enough to take a bullet for. Not when it ain't my fight."

Her face lost its pretty smile. "A hundred a month, then. It's my final offer."

I'd never made a hundred a month in my life, and might never again have the chance. "Why me, ma'am? You could get most anyone for that kind o' money."

"I have a dozen men who know how to use a gun, but what I don't have is someone to lead them. Billy tells me you were in the war?"

"I was in the war. Why?"

"What was your rank?"

"Sergeant, when I came out."

She nodded as if expecting the answer. "That's why I want you, Mr. Hawkins. You already know how to lead men in battle."

"Are you so certain there's going to be a fight?"

"No, not certain. But if it comes to it, I want my men ready."

I never claimed to be smart, but I know enough to not stick my hand in a rattlesnake's mouth. "No. I'm sorry, ma'am, but no. An' that's my final answer."

Her face flushed and her jaw set hard. She started to say something, changed her mind, and turned away. She climbed back onto the wagon seat. "Let's go, Dave," she said. "We're wasting our time here."

The old man next to her—Dave, I guess—snapped the reins and clicked his tongue, starting the wagon down the street. As they passed the saloon I started to turn back to my work, but stopped when three men stepped out of the saloon. All three men rode for the Rocking M. They watched Beth and her men pass, then climbed onto their horses and rode hell-bent for election out of town, off toward the Rocking M.

Beth and her men seemed to pay them no mind, an' I tried to do the same. Over the next hour I finished with the wagon, and started on the mare. I'd not worked on her before, but Red had given me fair warning.

Generally, if a horse is tamed enough to ride, it's tame enough to be shoed. Now and again you come across a horse that's still too wild, and those you leave be or put in a shoeing pen. Red wouldn't touch a horse like that, an' didn't even have a pen.

Well and good. But there's another kind of horse that's sneaky mean. If you're on your guard they're gentle as any lapdog, but let your attention slip away for even a moment, and like as not they'll kick a slat out of you.

According to Red, that mare would kick if given any chance at all, so I took care not to give her any chance. What Red didn't mention was biting. I had a rope on the mare, and tied her head down fairly close, but that didn't stop her a bit.

Either I didn't tie the knot proper, or she pulled it loose with her teeth, but somehow she got her head free. I had her right front leg between my legs, cutting down the hoof, when some God almighty big teeth nipped me in the hind-quarters. I yelped and jumped, calling that mare a few names that'd make a muleskinner blush.

She stood there looking at me out of sad old eyes, acting like she'd done nothing wrong. After tying the rope again,

I limped to the back of the smithy and dropped my drawers, then spent a minute trying to twist my head around enough to look at my own arse.

I'd been wearin' a leather apron that wrapped most of the way around, and the mare's teeth got mostly that and not much of me. But she'd still drawn a bit of blood, and it hurt like hell.

Red had a bottle of horse liniment sitting on a shelf, and lackin' anything better I poured a dollop of that on a rag and slapped it on my butt. Bad as the bite hurt, that liniment hurt worse, and I let go a few words that I'd forgotten I knew.

When the pain eased a bit, I pulled my pants back up, shoved a rag down there to stop what bleeding there was, and went back over to the mare. I put shoes on her all the way around and led her into a stall, promising myself Red could do the job next time she was brought in.

No work remained that couldn't wait awhile, so I decided the saloon could use another customer. Only, I hadn't more'n stepped outside when twenty Rocking M riders came galloping in, Neal Pierce at the front.

Beth Alison and her men were still in town, going from store to store, but when the Rocking M men showed at the edge of town somebody shouted a warning and the Reverse Box E men came together outside the mercantile. Beth Alison was inside, but she came out and stood right in front of her men, watching Neal Pierce and his riders come.

Pierce jerked his horse to a cruel stop in front of Beth, and his men fanned out behind him. Me, I was too far away to hear any of the words, but it was plain Pierce was yelling and Beth was giving it right back.

For a time it looked like the shooting was going to start right then and there. Then Pierce jerked his horse's head around and spurred him toward the saloon, his men following.

Beth and her men loaded up the wagon with supplies and rode out, but Billy broke loose and trotted his paint over to where I was standing. "Looks like the wolf got loose," he said. "Pierce told Beth not to stretch another foot of wire, else he'd rip it all from the ground. She told him to try it and be damned.

"I wish you'd change your mind about workin' for her, Ben. I talked it over with the boys, and there ain't none of us had real shootin' trouble before. Won't none of us back down, but it'd sure be nice to have an old hand to look to."

"Damn it, Billy, I told your boss lady no, and I'm tellin' you the same thing. I had hopes all this would blow over, but it's starting to look like a war brewing, Billy, and I want no part of it.

"When the shooting starts, men are going to get killed on both sides, and I like living. Best thing you can do is get out while you can."

A few cold raindrops fell, raising puffs of dust. "Nothin' worse than a winter rain," Billy said. "Hope it holds off till we reach the bunkhouse."

He looked down at me. "I can't do it, Ben. Maybe it's foolish, but I hired on saying I'd stick it out, and I got to do it. Might be I'm a fool, but it's how I feel."

"Can't nobody answer that question but you, Billy. I've stuck things out for worse reasons."

"I reckon. Well, so long, Ben. Be seein' you."

Billy rode out and for a time I stood there, lookin' after him. The rain started falling harder, though from the clouds it didn't look to be something that would last long.

It didn't. By the time I'd slipped on my jacket and closed the door to the smithy, the rain was already easing up.

Going over to the saloon, I had two beers and half a dozen pickled eggs for lunch. The saloon was full of Rocking M riders, though Johnny wasn't among them. Hank Collins stood at the bar, saw me, and the hate in his eyes was an ugly thing. But he turned away and didn't look back, so I ignored him.

Brice Campbell and Neal Pierce were sitting at a table over near the window, and when I went to the bar for my second beer and three more pickled eggs, Brice called me over. Taking eggs and beer over to the table, I sat down.

"Don't know how you can eat those damned eggs," Campbell said. "They sour my stomach for a week."

"Don't seem to bother me," I said. "Besides, you ate the stew they serve here?"

"I see your point," he said. "Hell, I come here to drink, anyway. I'll do my eating at the ranch."

Pierce sipped his beer. "Hawkins, isn't that your name?"

"Sure. Ben Hawkins."

"Looks like you were right to turn down the job I offered. That Alison woman won't budge, and I can't let her put up more wire."

"Why not?"

Pierce made a face. "Hell, man, you're a cattleman, you should know the answer to that. This is free range. Always has been, always will be.

"Cattle here have to walk a good piece for graze and water. Start fencing it off and they'll die."

"You mean your'n will die. I reckon Beth Alison will have the water and graze on the inside of the fence."

"Damn it, Hawkins, I've been running cattle over these plains for fifteen years. I'm not going to lose them just because some fool woman bought up enough land to let her fence off the whole damned river.

"Hell, she don't even claim to own the river! But stringing barbed wire so the cattle can't get to it amounts to the same thing, you ask me. What am I supposed to do?"

"You're askin' the wrong man," I said. "You want the truth, I think wire is the comin' thing, but I can see your point. Might be you should talk it over with Mrs. Alison. Maybe you can come to an understanding."

"An understanding? I settled this land, Hawkins. When I came here the Comanche were still on the warpath, and for every Indian there were two rustlers.

"But I built a ranch, by God. I own ten head of cattle for each and every one Beth Alison has. Her and all the other damned nesters put together.

"They're squatters, Hawkins. They come in late, after the danger was gone, and now they're trying to fence me out. I won't stand for it."

"Like I said, I see your point, but sometimes coming first don't matter much. I seen other men lose ranches for pretty much the same reason. You come along first, fight the hard fights, but you don't bother to buy up the land nor file on the best water because you figure you already own them.

"I knew a man, worked for him almost five years, who bought his land from the Spanish. Had a deed that'd take a man a week to read. For ten years the law said he owned the land, then some yahoo changed the law, and suddenly he didn't own nothing. He had plenty of cattle and no cash, and before he could make a move, his land was split twenty ways and sold to hell and gone. Hell, Pierce, maybe in your place I'd do the same thing. Might be you'll even win. But then what?"

"I'll win," he said. "And when it's over I'll own every inch of land and every drop of water for twenty miles in every direction. I'll buy it fair if they'll sell, or I'll buy it with bullets if they won't. But in the end I'll own it all.

"You were well to stay clear, Hawkins. Sure as hell is hot, Beth Alison won't stop stretching wire, and I won't back up an inch. The next wire that goes up, I turn Campbell and his men loose."

I looked to Brice. "Sounds to me like you'll be the one on the line."

"It's my job," he said. "I'm a range detective, and what I

do will stand up in any court. Mr. Pierce says run the nesters out, and I'll do it."

"What if they fight instead of run?"

"Then they're fools. I'm good at my job, Hawkins. Run or fight, it makes me no nevermind."

"There'll be blood on the land."

"There usually is. But it won't be yours, and I'll see to it that it ain't mine. Sometimes that's all you can do.

"By the way, I'm supposed to give you a message. Johnny said to tell you he'd be in one day this week. He says he'll buy the beer."

I smiled. "Tell him to hurry along. I'd drink with the devil himself if he'd do the buying."

Shoving the empty beer glass away, I stood up. "Well, keep yourself out of trouble, Brice. I'd best get back to work."

Walking back over to the smithy, I stoked the forge and worked the bellows a minute, then slid in a strip of iron to heat. There was trouble coming to Comanche Creek, sure as hell. And when trouble comes, folks have to choose sides or stay out of the picture altogether. Me, I meant to stay clear.

I had a good job, even if it was part time. I had a roof over my head and a saloon right across the street. It mightn't be much, but it was a damned sight better than being shot at.

CHAPTER 5

WHEN THE SHOOTING did start, word of it trickled into Comanche Creek a piece at a time. Five or six days after Beth Alison and Neal Pierce had words in front of the mercantile, an old man who lived just across the Pecos came into town, lookin' for a drink and a good time. He found both and talked plenty.

He said he'd been visiting over to the Reverse Box E when some of the cowhands brought a man in belly down over his horse. His name was Bob Winthrop, and he'd been out riding the wire. When he hadn't shown up at the bunkhouse on time, some men went out looking.

They found him dead. He'd been wrapped in barbed wire and dragged to death. Two of the Reverse Box E hands quit right on the spot.

Other reports of shootings drifted in the same way, but it seemed to still be an on-again, off-again thing, with neither side really doing much damage to the other. To me that meant Brice Campbell hadn't been turned loose proper yet.

Most folks will tell you a range detective is just a fancy name for a hired killer. Might be all who hire on as range detectives ain't that way, but enough are to make most men wary of crossing them. Brice Campbell seemed a decent enough man, but he'd the name of being ruthless in a fight.

Over to the saloon, men talked about him often, and I heard it said he'd killed as many men by laying up for them with a rifle as he had up close an' honest. I didn't doubt it for a minute.

Brice was the kind of man who'd buy you a drink, stake you with his last dollar, or stand right next to you come trouble. But if you were on the other side of the trouble, he'd be a different story. His job was to clear the range of rustlers, suspected rustlers, or anybody at all who gave the big ranchers trouble.

And Brice was good at it. He wouldn't give a damn whether he shot a man with warnin' or without, and he wouldn't call anything he did murder . . . not even wrapping a man in barbed wire and dragging him to death. To Brice, and most others, the big ranchers were the law, and anything he did to uphold their interests was just.

The truth is, there wasn't all that much to be done around the smithy most days. Barely enough to keep Red occupied, much less the both of us, so generally I had four days out of every week free and clear. I couldn't remember ever havin' so much time to myself in my life.

Sure, I'd ridden the grub line, and gone long weeks, and once nearly three months, without work. But that was different. Every day I'd be looking for work, worrying about work, and riding over hell and gone trying to find work.

Now I was making enough to keep body and soul together, I had a roof, and as much as two dollars free and clear at the end of each week. It left me wondering what to do with those four days.

Not that I didn't already have ideas, mind you. I drank a bit, played cards a bit, sat in the saloon and lied about things I'd done and places I'd been to other cowboys or townfolk who lied to me in turn. Yes, sir, for the most part it was a mighty pleasant way to spend a winter.

But after a while it got to making me nervous. It didn't seem right to have so much free time, if you want to know. So I went to looking for odd work on those days, and pretty soon I was busier than you'd believe.

A quiet month passed, and in that month I painted buildings, patched roofs, cleaned up after horses, and replaced half the boards along the sidewalk. Most towns, it's the marshal's job to keep the sidewalk repaired, but Comanche Creek didn't have a marshal, nor did it want one.

Pretty soon I had near twenty dollars put aside, and it was then I took up with Ruby Kieler, a redheaded gal who worked at the saloon. I never was much with women, and there wasn't no doubt in my mind she was intending to go through my money as fast as I made it, but I couldn't complain if she was.

Ruby was twenty-eight or so, and the prettiest of the five who worked there. I bought her a dress and a few doodads she seemed to like, and we'd spend long hours up in her room. Some days she'd be busy, or I'd be in the mood for a game of five-card draw, and then we'd go about our own business with no words said. Other times, though, we'd hole up in her room with a bottle and poke the day away.

The shooting between the Rocking M and the Reverse Box E had died off again, mostly because word came that Beth Alison had stopped stringing barbed wire. Nobody knew if it was true or not, but for several weeks there was no word of any shootings.

The Rocking M boys came to town often, but they didn't speak about it much. Brice Campbell did say he allowed things were just standing still for a time, but he reckoned they'd pick up soon. That was on one Saturday night, but by the next he was keyed up, and mad to boot.

"Alison stopped laying wire," he said, "so Mr. Pierce told us to lay off. He figured she come to realize she couldn't win and was backing down.

"I told him it wasn't time to quit, that she was likely getting ready to push at us, but he wouldn't hear it. Day before yesterday I sent a couple of men riding over that way to make sure they wasn't putting up more wire, and they got jumped by eight or ten men."

"Was there shooting?"

"Damn right, there was shooting! They opened up on

my boys without a word. Killed one man right off and put a bullet in the other, though he managed to slip away. You know what he told us, Hawkins? He said the man doing most of the shooting wore a sombrero and rode a big, buttermilk-colored horse."

"So? Do you know him?"

"I know him. I wasn't sure, but I rode over and laid up on a hill till I got a good look. He's a fellow named Jim Macklin. Rio Grande Jim, they used to call him."

"Oh, hell, I've heard of him. Used to run with a big bunch of men. They spent most of their time in Mexico, but they'd cross the border and steal a whole damn herd of horses or cattle and have them back across the Rio Grande before anyone could say a word."

"That's him. Him and his bunch ran into some Rangers one night and got shot to pieces, but it looks like he's still around."

"How'd he come to be working for Beth Alison?"

Brice threw a shot of whiskey down his throat. "Now that's a question, ain't it, Hawkins? However it come to be, it's war now. Macklin's a rustler, pure and proven. Ain't no way Mr. Pierce can let him stay around."

"Are you sure Mrs. Alison knows what he is? Might be he just drifted in, asking for work, and she hired him on."

"It might be, but if that's the case why'd he shoot up my men? Besides, it don't matter now. Macklin's riding for the Reverse Box E, and that means war."

Two weeks passed after that with little happening. Then came a Tuesday afternoon toward the end of January when all hell broke loose, pulling me right along with it.

It was cold, near freezing, and that's a rare thing so far south. Not that I minded. I was spending the day with Ruby, and one thing about her, she believes in plenty of covers on her bed. She had a tub right there in her room, and after a quick bath we crawled under the covers, laughing and carrying on like kids.

Ruby might have been ten or fifteen pounds on the heavy side, but to me that made her more pleasin', and for a couple of hours I didn't care what the weather was or if summer ever came. Afterward, we huddled under the covers for a time, Ruby on her side with her bare breasts pressing hard against me.

Then she slipped out of bed and into a frilly robe, thinking to go downstairs to the bar and bring us both a beer and a sandwich. She went down and came back up, but she hadn't been in bed more than five minutes when somebody knocked on the door.

Ruby yelled out, askin' who it was, and the voice answering said he was Jeff Grimes, and that he rode for the Reverse Box E. I told him to come on in, and he did. Me and Ruby were both sitting up in the bed.

Grimes came through the door and his eyes locked right on Ruby, and I could see he'd lost all thought of what he came to tell me.

Ruby smiled, pulled the covers up to her chin. Only then did Jeff Grimes look at me. "You Ben Hawkins?"

"That's right."

"You're Billy Martin's friend?"

"Sure. We rode into Comanche Creek together last fall."

"Well, Billy caught a bullet early this morning. He asked me to come see you. Wants to know if you can ride out to the ranch when you get to it."

I sat up straighter. "How bad is he?"

Grimes shrugged. "He got hit below the knee. It was a big bullet and hit the bone square on. His leg's sure a bloody mess."

"What about a doctor?"

"Mrs. Alison sent for one straight off. He hadn't shown up yet when I left."

"Well, *hell*! You going straight back?"

He nodded. "Pick up a bottle, an' I'm gone."

"Tell Billy I'll be out directly."

"Sure thing."

Grimes went out the door, closing it behind him. The jingle of his spurs was loud as he walked to the stairs. Swinging my legs from the bed and onto the floor, I began pulling on my longjohns. Ruby reached over and ran her fingernails lightly down my back. "You ain't going now, are you, Ben?"

"I reckon. Billy's asking."

"Can't it wait till morning?"

"No, it's best I go now. I can get there a good bit before dark if I push."

"What about me?"

Pulling my pants over my longjohns, I fished deep in a pocket and came out with a gold eagle. It was too much and I knew it, but what the hell? Ruby caught it on the flip.

"Buy yourself somethin' pretty," I said. "You can wear it for me when I get back."

"I'll save it just for you, honey."

Getting on the last of my clothes, I went downstairs to the bar. My head was a bit light from lying in bed all morning, drinking and whatnot with Ruby, so I made a big sandwich from a tray of beef and ate it on the way over to the smithy.

Red was bending an iron rod into fancy shapes, just beginning work on a fireplace screen. I could do such work, but not so fast as Red, and not without making more mistakes along the way. I told him where I was headed and why. He hammered on a minute, then looked up.

"You be careful, Ben. Don't go getting yourself caught in the middle of anything, hear?"

"Yes, sir. Only, me and Billy rode together. Guess I got to go."

"Not sayin' you don't. Just be careful, is all."

"I'll do it."

Saddling my horse, I took the time to roll a smoke, then rode out. Two hours of light remained when I came in sight of the house. Half a dozen riders came along to meet me, all holding rifles. I explained what I wanted and they let me on through.

I half expected to find Billy in the bunkhouse, but Beth Alison had him up to the main house in a fine bed. It was likely ruined permanent from the blood. Beth Alison was standing in the doorway, and a man I took to be a doctor was just starting to unwrap the crude bandage someone had applied to Billy's leg.

Billy looked right at me, but his eyes seemed flat, and it took him a second to recognize me. "Ben, is that you?"

"It's me, Billy."

Billy shook his head. "Doc. Doc, you hear me?"

The doctor stopped his doings for a moment. "What is it, son?"

"Leave me be. I want to talk to Ben before you go messing with my leg."

"This needs to be looked at right away."

"A minute . . . a . . . what in hell did you give me, doc? Feel like my head's full of bees and my mouth's full of cotton."

"Laudanum. Morphine would have been better, but I don't have any in stock. I gave you a healthy dose of laudanum, though. It should have dulled the pain by now."

"Dulled me, is what it done. Now let me talk to Ben while I still can."

The doctor looked at Beth, who nodded. "Do you want us to leave?" she asked.

Billy nodded. They went on out and I sat down on a chair near the bed. Billy's eyes closed for so long I thought maybe he'd passed out. Then he opened them and looked at me. I saw his eyes focus.

"How'd it happen, Billy?"

Billy shook his head. "That new fellow, Macklin's his name. Beth hired him on and he up and took over. Him and the others he hired in turn. Led us right into an ambush. Don't matter now, though.

"Ben, are we friends? I mean, we worked together and rode together, but are we real friends?"

"You know we are, Billy."

"Then I got something to ask you. You ain't gonna like it, but I'm askin' anyway. Macklin figures a woman can't run a ranch, and he's plain taken over. Or trying to. If he stays any longer he'll hire more men and it'll be too late.

"You got to help Beth. You got to, Ben. Take the job she offered. She'll put you in charge, and then things'll work out. I know it. But you got to take the job."

Billy's face was beaded with sweat, and I allowed the laudanum was wearin' off. "Damn it, Billy, you know how I feel about this. You got no right to ask me that. No right at all."

"I know I ain't, Ben. But I'm still asking. Will you do it? Beth'll lose everything if you don't."

"Billy—"

"I'm askin', Ben."

I swore then. I swore at Billy, I swore at Beth Alison, and I swore at myself. "All right, Billy. If Mrs. Alison still wants me, I'll take the job. But that don't mean I'll run out and fight Brice Campbell and his men."

"Just so long as you take the job. It'll work out, Ben. With you here, it'll all work out."

"Maybe so, Billy. Maybe so. Now lay back and let me get the doc in here."

Billy just nodded. Going to the doorway, I yelled for the doctor. He came in, gave Billy more laudanum, then took the bandage off his leg. He hadn't looked at the wound for more than a few seconds before standing up. He stripped off his coat and started rolling up his sleeves.

"You had better get two or three strong men in here," he said to Mrs. Alison. "This boy's leg has to be amputated."

Billy seemed not to hear. I'd seen amputations by the

score in the war. At Gettysburg, I'd seen piles of arms and legs higher than a man's head outside the surgeon's tents, and the screaming from inside made a man pray to God he never had to go in there. A shudder ran through me at the thought.

"Are you certain sure, Doc. Ain't there no other way?"

He looked me right in the eye. "The bone is shattered. I couldn't begin to put it together again, nor could I find all the bone splinters and lead fragments. The wound is already showing the first signs of gangrene, and if I don't amputate right now, this boy will be dead within twenty-four hours. Does that answer your question?"

"Yes, sir. Tell me what's needed and I'll see it gets done."

CHAPTER 6

THE DOCTOR BEGAN digging instruments from his bag. He had Mrs. Alison boil a pan of hot water, and told me to bring in the men to help hold Billy down. Two big cowboys were standing on the porch, smoking cigarettes and wait-ing to see how Billy was doing. I hauled them into the bed-room, and we surrounded the bed.

The doc took a big bottle of laudanum from his bag and gave Billy more than I'd have wanted to swallow. Billy gagged a little, looked up at me. "Johnny was there, Ben. He was shootin' right along with the rest. Saw him with my own eyes."

Within a minute the laudanum began taking effect, and Billy's eyes went blank.

I'd never seen a man's leg taken off before, though I'd seen the results plenty of times. After Gettysburg, the wounded were hauled south in wagons, and the line stretched a solid fifteen miles. Hundreds, maybe thou-sands, lost arms or legs, and they were the lucky ones.

So while I'd never actually seen a leg come off, I'd heard plenty about it, told by men who'd been on the wrong end of the knife. "It ain't as bad as you'd think," a soldier told me. "Didn't take them more'n a minute to slice my leg off and send me on my way."

I knew he was right. It was said some doctors could take off a leg or an arm in forty seconds flat. Part of the reason for speed was to keep up with the hundreds of soldiers waiting for help after a big battle, and part was to lessen blood loss and hold shock to a minimum.

Least that's what I was told, and believe me, we talked

about it plenty. What a soldier feared most was taking a bullet in the gut, because that meant a slow death and nothing the surgeons could do. But right next in line was the fear of losing an arm or a leg.

With the laudanum in full effect, the doc went to work. He cut through the meat of Billy's leg several inches above the wound, leaving a large flap of skin hanging free on one side. Then he sewed off some big arteries and veins, and cut through them.

The bone was already shattered by the bullet, but he sawed through it above that, leaving a smooth, flat edge of bone. Then he covered the wound with the flap of skin and sewed that down, leaving one edge open so the leg could drain. He washed the wound, covered it with a carbolic spray, and bandaged it with a clean cloth.

I didn't have a pocket watch, but it couldn't have been more than five minutes from the time he started work on the leg until the job was done. The laudanum had done its work well, and Billy didn't thrash about but once, and that weakly.

That aside, I knew the next few weeks would be the rough ones for Billy. Losing an arm or leg is a hard thing, and many men can't handle it. More than one soldier who came out of the surgeon's tent with less than he had going in waited his chance and finished the job with a bullet through the head.

"It went well enough," the doctor said, "but I don't like the looks of his leg. He'd be better off in town."

"Who'd look after him?" I asked.

"He has no friends in town?"

"No, sir."

"Then I guess he'll have to stay here. I'd look after him if I could, but my patients are scattered over thirty square miles, so I'm gone most of the time.

"I'll stop by whenever I can, and I'll leave a bottle of

laudanum. Go easy on giving it to him, though. Sometimes a man gets started on laudanum and can't stop."

"Yes, sir," I said. "I've seen it happen."

"He'll probably sleep for two or three hours, and when he wakes up he'll be in a good deal of pain. Get him to bear all he can, and use the laudanum as a last resort."

Mrs. Alison asked what she owed him, and he said twenty dollars. She paid him without question. He re-packed his instruments and left. I'd been so intent on Billy that I hadn't even caught the doctor's name. Mrs. Alison said it was Thomas Hall.

"If you have a few minutes, ma'am," I said, "I'd like to talk to you."

She nodded. "Would you like a cup of coffee, Mr. Hawkins? I believe there may be something to eat still on the stove."

"That sounds good, ma'am. I haven't eaten since noon."

She led me into a big kitchen, poured a cup of coffee, and handed it to me. I sat down at the table and she brought over a plate of beans, a big chunk of fresh-baked bread, and several slices of salt pork.

I ate quickly, shoved back from the table a little. "Do you mind if I smoke, ma'am?"

"No, of course not. Go ahead, please."

Rolling a cigarette, I struck a match and touched it to the end of the paper. Mrs. Alison gave me an ashtray, and I flicked ashes into it. "Billy asked me to go to work for you, ma'am."

"Are you going to?"

"Depends."

"On what, Mr. Hawkins?"

"Mostly on what you aim to do, and on how you'll let me handle things."

"I'm not sure I understand."

"I mean, ma'am, are you bound and determined to have a war with Pierce, or are you open to negotiatin'?"

"Negotiate how?"

"Neal Pierce came in here early, ma'am, and he went through hell building his herd. You can't hardly blame him for wanting to get those cattle to water."

"It's not the water that concerns me, Mr. Hawkins, it's the grass. This area has too many cattle and the land will soon be overgrazed. The grass between here and the river is the best, but even it can't withstand too much pressure. I intend to fence it off, Mr. Hawkins."

"Do you own all the land you're fencin' in?"

"No, I do not. I own most of it, but here and there I've had my men put up fence across free range in order to connect sections of mine."

"Would you be willing to leave a couple of sections open all the way to the river?"

"So Neal Pierce can still water his cattle in the Pecos?"

"That's right."

She didn't answer for a couple of minutes. "It seems a reasonable request," she said at last. "I never wanted to put Pierce out of business. I want only to save grass for my cattle."

"Well and good, ma'am. That'll be my first step, then."

"Do you think Pierce will settle for a strip of land?"

I smiled. "Ma'am, I just don't know. The only way to find out is to ask, and that's what I'll do."

"What else do you want?"

"I want the say-so. You can fire me at any time, but whilst I'm workin', I want to do things my way. You tell us to string wire, fine, we'll string it, but my way. I want to hire and fire, and if there's fightin' to be done, my word is final."

"That all?"

"Yes, ma'am. I expect it's enough."

She turned away, looked out the window. There wasn't much light left in the sky. "There may be one problem, Mr. Hawkins. I hired a man named Jim Macklin."

"Yes, ma'am. That's another thing. I want him fired."

"That's just it. I told him he was fired when they brought Billy back. He laughed at me and said he'd leave when he was good and ready."

"All right. I'll handle Macklin. Where is he?"

"He rode out with two other men not long before you arrived. I don't think he's returned yet. What will you do?"

"I'll fire him."

"And if he won't leave?"

"He'll leave, ma'am. I won't give him a choice."

She smiled. "If you're going to work for me, Mr. Hawkins, there is one thing I demand."

"Ma'am?"

"Exactly. Stop calling me that. It makes me feel old. Call me Beth. I insist."

"All right, ma'am, I mean, Beth. I reckon you'd best call me Ben, or just Hawkins. Can't remember nobody ever calling me mister for long."

"Then it's a deal, Ben. Shake on it."

I took her hand in mine and shook it. She had strong hands, roughened a little by hard work. That's a fine thing in anyone, man or woman.

"We need to talk a bit more, ma'—I mean, Beth, but it can wait. I think now I'd best go down to the bunkhouse and wait for Macklin to show up. I don't suppose you have a short-barreled shotgun in the house?"

"As a matter of fact, I have."

She led me into a room on the other side of the house. A big desk filled the room, backed by a leather-covered chair. A large painting of a cattle roundup hung on one wall, and a wide gun cabinet stood against another. The cabinet held half a dozen rifles of various makes and models, along with three shotguns.

"This was my husband's den," she said. "I've left it exactly as it was."

Most of the rifles were fancy models with pretty engraving on the stocks and gold-filled etchings on the barrels and receivers. Same with the shotguns. But on the right-hand side of the cabinet stood an 1873 Winchester lever-action rifle, .44 caliber, and a double-barreled Greener 10-gauge shotgun.

The stocks and forearms of both weapons were nicked and scarred, and the barrels scratched by rough use. Picking up the shotgun, I broke it open and looked down the barrels. They were clean and well-oiled.

Opening a drawer at the bottom of the cabinet, I found it filled with ammunition of every kind needed for the weapons. I dug out a box of 10-gauge shells, slipped two into the shotgun, dropped half a dozen more into my coat pocket.

"It's funny you should choose that shotgun," Beth said. "It was my husband's favorite. He called it his 'business gun.' Anytime he suspected trouble was near, he would load that shotgun and the Winchester."

"What about all these others?" I asked.

"They were mostly gifts from friends or business associates. James said he'd feel like a fool taking one hunting. He didn't approve of fancy weapons."

"I reckon me an' your husband had something in common. I favor a plain look myself. Getting the job done is the thing, an' no amount of gold foofaraw ever helped with that."

Beth crossed her arms and looked down at the floor. After a time she looked back up at me. "Why are you doing this?"

"What? You mean working for you?"

"Yes. And taking it on yourself to get rid of Macklin. He's a very dangerous man. You might be killed. So why?"

"There's no mystery about it. Billy asked me to help, and him laying there with a stump where his leg oughta be . . . Guess I'm going soft, but me an' Billy rode together, and it wasn't in me to say no."

"You'd risk being killed because you and Billy rode together?"

"Ma'am—I mean, Beth, I can't see where there is a better reason. Every time a cowboy leaves the bunkhouse and goes looking for cattle he's risking his life, and that for thirty or forty dollars a month. Might be I shouldn't have said yes, and truth be known, it might be I'd rather have said no."

"But what if you're killed?"

"Then you're on your own. But I don't expect I'll be killed today. Macklin might be a dangerous man, but he don't know I'm comin', and I won't let him get set. Might be he'll come back on me later, but I'll worry about that when the times comes."

"You must be a very brave man, Ben."

I smiled. "Don't you believe it. Just thinking about going down to the bunkhouse ties a knot right down where I live. No, I wouldn't call myself brave at all.

"Fact is, I never thought much of pulling courage from a bottle, but once trouble is over, well, that's another thing, if you catch my meaning."

She nodded. "I'll have a drink waiting when you come back, Ben. And thanks."

"You're welcome, Beth. Make it a tall drink, will you?"

Taking a deep breath, I walked out of the house and toward the bunkhouse. Before I was halfway there, three riders came tearing in. They looped their reins around a rail of the corral and went into the bunkhouse. I'd hoped to be inside the bunkhouse, waiting for Macklin, but it looked like he'd beaten me to it.

The sun dropped below the horizon, and dusk swept across the land. Shifting the heavy shotgun from one hand to the other, I wiped both palms on my coat, then walked down to the bunkhouse.

I wondered how it was that some men never learn a damn thing. I'd come through a war in one piece, and swore when it was over I'd never go near trouble again. Now here I was, shotgun in hand, walking right into another war.

"Ben Hawkins," I said aloud, "you are one dumb son of a bitch."

That said, I went on walking, proving to myself just how dumb I really was.

CHAPTER 7

REACHING THE BUNKHOUSE, I stepped through the door. Five men were stretched out on bunks, and three others sat at a table shoved up against the far wall. Since they were the only ones still wearing boots, it seemed likely one of those three would be Macklin.

That table was maybe forty feet from the door, and holding that Greener 10-gauge down against my leg, I walked straight toward it. When I was halfway there, the man on the far side of the table looked up. "Who the hell are you?" he asked.

I kept walking, stopping right up against the table. "Are you Macklin?"

"That I am. What's it to you?"

"My name is Ben Hawkins. Beth Alison just hired me on as foreman. My first chore is to see you're sent packing."

Rio Grande Jim was a man above average size, and a handsome, blond, smiling man, to boot. Right then he smiled at me. "You run me off, you got to run my friends off, too, Hawkins. You think you're up to the three of us?"

Fighting Macklin was one thing. Fighting all three of them was something else again. The only way to do it was to get the edge. Without another word I swung the shotgun left, catching the man in the chair across his nose with the butt. He flipped over backward, and I swung back the other way, hitting the man on the right in the teeth. He screamed and hit the floor hard, his hands to his mouth.

The table was a small, flimsy affair, weighing no more than fifteen pounds or so, and I jerked it out of the way with one hand. Macklin was on his feet, his Colt all the way

55

out of the holster, when I shoved the twin barrels of the shotgun hard into his stomach and cocked both hammers.

"What happens next is up to you," I said. "It don't matter a tinker's damn to me."

The Colt in his hand was only inches from my gut, and if he pulled the trigger he'd have killed me sure. But if just one barrel of that shotgun went off he wouldn't live to see me fall. A 10-gauge is a fearful thing at any range, but having one shoved into your gut that way has to make you wish you were somewhere else.

But I'll say one thing for Macklin, he had his share of nerve. He wasn't liking that shotgun being where it was, but he didn't turn to jelly, neither. "It would almost be worth it to take you with me, Hawkins."

"Like I said, Macklin, I don't give a damn. But I'm getting tired of waiting, so make up your mind."

He looked me right in the eye for a minute, then smiled and let the Colt drop to the floor. "There'll be another time," he said.

"I hope not, Macklin. Best thing you can do is count this one as a loss an' go about your business."

"Might be I'll do just that, Hawkins. Might be I won't. Guess I'll have to think about it a spell."

"Fair enough. Only, do your thinking while you're riding. And take your friends with you."

The man on the left was still lying as he fell, and for a minute I thought he was dead. But when Macklin prodded him with the toe of his boot, the man groaned and opened his eyes. He looked up at me and anger flared on his face, but Macklin stopped it.

"Not now, Stu. Let's get outta here."

He helped the man to his feet, steadied him. Blood dripped steadily from a deep cut on the man's nose, and I'd seen enough broken noses to know his was busted proper.

The other fellow was still groaning and clutching at his

mouth, but he went along peaceful enough. He did pause at the door long enough to call me a "shumbish," the best he could do without the three teeth he'd left on the floor.

When they were gone, I looked around the bunkhouse. "Anybody else doubts who's in charge here, now's the time to put in your two cents' worth."

A tall, skinny man with long hair was sitting on a bunk, cutting away at his fingernails with a pocketknife. He spoke without looking up. "Mrs. Alison says you're the boss, then you're the boss. I was figuring on quittin' if Macklin stayed. Guess most of the others feel the same way."

A murmur of agreement ran through the bunkhouse, and then a man with dark hair stood up. He didn't look to be more than eighteen, but if he did the work he was hired to do, and if he carried a gun like a man, then his age didn't mean a thing.

"I hired on to do a job," he said, "but it's starting to look like a losing proposition. It ain't that I'm yellow, but I reckon it's time for me to look for other work."

"Your choice," I said, "and likely the smart one. Anybody else feel the same?"

One other man stood up. "Guess I got to side with Danny. No offense . . . you said your name was Hawkins, didn't you?"

"That's right."

"Well, no offense, Hawkins, but that ambush today kind of did me in. If it's all the same to you, I'll stay the night and leave come daylight."

"Fine. One thing, though. I'll take it hard if I see either of you riding for the Rocking M."

"You don't have to worry about that. I want a job where I can tend cattle without dodging bullets."

"Just so we understand each other. As for the rest of you, do your thinking tonight. Come morning, I want to know who's here to stay, and who ain't."

I walked back up to the house and knocked.

Beth came to the door. "There's no need of knocking," she said. "As foreman, you'll need access to the house at all times. In fact, I think you should use my husband's den. There's a room right next to it where you can sleep."

"I've never slept in as fine a house, but it might be a good idea. If I'm going to be in charge of the men, it might be a good thing to stay up here. You get to know a man too well, and you have trouble taking orders from him. That's one of the first things they learnt us in the army. The enlisted men sleep one place, the officers another, and that's the reason."

"It makes a certain kind of sense, I suppose. Ben, I'm going to sit with Billy for a while, but do you want some supper?"

"Do you have a cook?"

"No."

"Who does the cooking for the hands?"

"I do. I had a man who cooked for them, but he quit about two weeks ago."

"Be best if I hired another, if I can find one. We need a cook out on the trail, someone who can also lend a hand if there's trouble.

"Talking about it is making me hungry again, but I think I'll pass. I need to ride back to Comanche Creek and take care of a few things."

"Do you have to go tonight?"

"Be best. Red Heinlin will expect me to work some tomorrow, and it wouldn't be right to not show up without giving him warning. And I have a few things in town to pick up."

"All right. But come back as soon as you can. I'll feel better knowing you're here."

"I don't expect there'll be more trouble tonight, Beth. Pierce seems to be holding his men in. Likely that'll change if we keep stringing wire, but for now he'll sit tight.

"But that's another thing. Tomorrow afternoon I intend

to ride over to the Rocking M and have a sit-down talk with Pierce. Might be we can iron things out."

"Perhaps. Tonight, though, I have something for you."

"What's that?"

Beth walked over to a small cabinet against the den wall and opened the doors. The cabinet was well stocked with liquor and glasses. She opened a bottle, poured three fingers in a glass, handed it to me.

"You said to make it a tall one."

"Yes, ma'am, I did. I'd near forgot."

Most often, I drank whatever rotgut was handy, but now and again I'd tossed an extra four bits on the bar to get a taste of something fine. Not much of it had been up to what Beth handed me, though. I said as much.

"We never had as much money or as many cattle as Neal Pierce," Beth said, "but we had enough. My husband liked the finer things in life, and was willing to pay for them. He had that whiskey brought in from Ireland.

"It was twenty-five years old when he bought it, and now it's almost three years older."

"It's sat there since he died?"

"James didn't die, Ben, he was killed."

"Killed?"

"Yes. He was shot in a foolish barroom fight by a cowboy he'd never seen before. They were both drinking, and one thing led to another.

"He was a good man, but a hothead, and sometimes he drank too much. I didn't mind any of that because he always treated me like a lady, but I don't think I'll ever forgive him for getting himself killed."

Beth's eyes were wet, and I stood there not knowing what to say or do. All I could think of to say was "I'm sorry."

"Yes, so am I, Ben. But there's nothing to be done about it. James is dead, and I'm left to run this ranch. That's just the way it is.

"Now, if you're going to Comanche Creek, you'd better be on your way. It's a long ride, and you'll want to get some sleep tonight."

"All I can, but I'll be back tomorrow."

I went out into the night, feeling like a fool for getting myself involved in something I wanted no part of, knowing I could back out, but knowing too that I wouldn't. It only made me feel more the fool.

Excepting the saloon, Comanche Creek was dead when I rode into town. Red had shut the smithy down long since, but I went in through a side door that was never locked. Once inside, I opened the main door and put my horse into a stall. Only after rubbing him down and giving him fresh hay and a bit of oats did I walk over to Red's house.

A lamp still shone in the window, so I knocked on the door. Red answered, wearing old work pants and no shirt, his suspenders pulled up over the top of his longjohns. I explained about Billy losing his leg and my taking on the job at the Reverse Box E.

Red stepped out onto the porch, looked up toward the sky. The stars were low and bright, and a crescent moon sat not far above the horizon. "I hate to lose you, Ben," he said. "You do fine work, and I'd hoped you'd stick awhile."

"Yes, sir, I got to liking it myself. Look, to be flat honest, working for the Reverse Box E ain't a thing I want to do. I'd a lot rather be down to the smithy, shaping iron."

"Then why did you take it on?"

" 'Cause of Billy, I guess. It's a hard thing to lose a leg, and Billy's still young. An' we rode together. . . . Damn it, Red, I don't know why I took it on. I don't know if I'm doing right, or just playing the fool."

"I can't answer that for you, Ben. All I can tell you is to do what feels right. If you get through it, come on back. Your job will be waiting."

"Thanks, Red. I 'preciate it."

Taking the time to clear my few belongings from the

small house Red had given me to sleep in, I walked down to the saloon. The tinny blare of the piano, the babble of voices, and the thick smoke came as a shock after the long, cool ride in the clear night. But outside some drafty bunkhouse, a saloon was the closest thing to home I'd had since the war.

Ruby was sittin' with a cowhand I didn't know, but when she saw me she smiled and waved. Thinking it might be my last night in town for a while, I burrowed in between two men at the bar and asked for a beer and a shot of whiskey.

A poker game was going on at a corner table, so I tossed down the whiskey and carried the beer over to watch. After a while one of the players quit and I sat down. I'd played maybe half a dozen hands when a pair of soft hands touched my shoulder. Looking up, I saw Ruby.

"Did you come for the cards, or for me?"

"Both," I said. "Thought I'd spend the night."

"How do you know I'm not going to be busy all night?"

"Figured you loved me enough to keep your nights open."

"You assume a lot, Ben Hawkins."

Tossing in the cards I held, I looked over my shoulder at Ruby. "No, ma'am, I don't. You got company for the night, just say so and I'll sleep elsewhere."

She frowned. "Sometimes I don't know what to make of you, Ben. When you're ready let me know."

"Guess I'll play cards for a spell. I'm kind of keyed up tonight."

Squeezing my shoulders, she walked away. She mightn't know what to make of me, but I didn't have her figured out neither. It seemed to me she was acting peculiar, like it was more than the money I spent on her that kept her interested in me.

Well, I'd known men who'd married up with saloon girls, and most often it worked out fine. It could be that Ruby was looking at me with marriage in mind. If so, she'd have to look again. Half the time I couldn't pay my own bar tab, let alone take on a wife.

No, sir. If Ruby was getting attached, it was time to be moving on. Might be working for the Reverse Box E wasn't such a bad thing after all.

CHAPTER 8

IT WAS MIDNIGHT by the time I finished playing cards. Counting my money while drinking a last beer, I found I'd come out near four dollars behind. Then again, I'd drunk several beers, so the loss wasn't all that great. Slipping the money into a pocket, I walked up the stairs to Ruby's room.

Rapping on the door, I waited until Ruby answered, then stepped inside. She was sitting in front of a mirror, running a brush through her long red hair. And I had to admit, she was a fine-looking woman.

Her eyes met mine in the mirror. "I was beginning to think you weren't coming up," she said.

"Guess the card game drug on some."

Ruby stood up and turned around. She was wearing a frilly blue gown, but it was open down the front, and there wasn't nothin' under it but her. She was a bit heavy in the hips, and had a little roll around back of her waist. But for all of that, Ruby was enough to make a poor old cowboy wish he never had to go back out on the range.

She kissed me, and after shucking my own clothes, we crawled into bed. For a time I forgot all about Beth Alison, Neal Pierce, and everything else in the world. Afterward, we propped ourselves against the pillows and drank beer. I rolled a cigarette for Ruby and another for myself.

Inhaling deep, I let the smoke trickle out. Ruby's body was hot, so I threw the covers off. She huddled over against me. It was then I told her about going to work for Beth Alison.

"I guess that means you won't be coming in as often," she said.

"I reckon not."

"I'll miss you."

"Me, or my money?"

"Both. I like you, Ben, I really do. But a girl has to earn a living."

I stabbed out my cigarette. "Ruby, can I ask you somethin' straight out?"

"Sure."

"Are you getting a case on me?"

She looked at me, no smile on her face or in her eyes. "Is that what you think?"

"It's crossed my mind."

"Ben, you asked straight, so I'll answer the same way. I meant it when I said I liked you. Not many men are as nice as you, and not many show me any kind of respect.

"But if you mean am I falling in love with you, no. I followed that road once, and I didn't like where it led. I like you, and I hope we're friends. If you were broke, I'd probably slip under the covers with you anyway, but I wouldn't make a habit of it. Does that answer your question?"

"Plain as could be. Reckon I feel the same way. Truth is, though, you had me worried for a time. Guess I never had a woman like me as a friend, or as anything else for that matter."

"That's hard to believe. Didn't you ever have a sweetheart?"

"Nope. I left home early on, then joined up and fit in the war. Been a cowhand ever since. Guess I never been around any women other than those at trail's end."

"You mean women like me?"

"Wasn't any of 'em like you, Ruby."

"That's sweet, Ben. It really is."

Ruby drifted off to sleep with her head on my shoulder, and after a while I pulled the covers up and did the same.

The rain pelting against the window woke me up not

long after dawn. Ruby was lying on my left arm, and I eased it from under her. My whole arm felt like a dead stick, with no feeling in it at all. After a minute it started tingling, then hurting for real.

I rubbed it until most of the tingling stopped, thought about getting up, decided against it, tried to go back to sleep. It was the need to visit the little house out back that made me slip from bed at last.

Pulling on my longjohns, pants, and boots, I went down the back stairs and outside. The rain was coming down just hard enough to wet a man, and the northwest wind was pushing it along pretty good. The dusty ground had turned to a half inch of mud, and the sky was low, gray, and angry. It didn't look like the weather would let up anytime soon.

Ruby was awake when I got back to her room, though she didn't look happy about it. "Might as well get up, darlin'," I said. "The day's half gone."

"Half gone, my arse. Cowboys may get up at dawn, but girls like me sleep till noon. Why don't you get out of those wet clothes and come back to bed?"

I grinned. "Can't say it ain't temptin', Ruby, but I'd best not. I crawl back between those sheets, and I might not crawl out again until tomorrow."

"Would that be so bad?"

"No, but I got things to do, and puttin' them off will just make 'em harder to do later on. Guess I'll get a bit of breakfast and some coffee in me, then get going."

"The bar's probably open," Ruby said. "They get in a pretty good breakfast crowd most days. The rain might slow things up."

"Hope not. Though I could use a shave and a bath, come to think of it."

Ruby sighed and swung her feet to the floor. "You run on out back and take care of the bath," she said. "I'll see to it that breakfast is ready when you come back up."

"Breakfast in bed?"

"Why not? You may be used to sitting under some tree and eating cold food, but not me."

I took my razor and the cleanest dirty clothes I had back to the shack where they kept the barrels. It was unlocked, so I went in, built a fire and pumped a washtub full of water and let it heat.

Soon as it was warm enough, I undressed and bathed. Then I shaved, leaving the mustache. I dressed and returned to Ruby's room, using the back stairs. She was back in bed, a big tray of bacon, eggs, and biscuits waiting. She'd also brought up a pot of coffee and a small jar of homemade jam.

Between the rain and Ruby's coaxing, it was near ten o'clock before I saddled my horse and rode out of town.

The sky stayed low and gray, but the rain had stopped, so I pointed my horse toward the Rocking M. When I reached the Rocking M I stopped over by the corral. Three cowboys were sitting on the top rail, watching a fourth trying his luck on a bucking, mouse-colored mustang.

One of them said I'd find Mr. Pierce out behind the house, so I looped the reins of my horse over a rail and walked around back. I found him and two other men digging a well forty feet from the back porch.

With pick and shovel they'd gone down twelve feet or so, and that was a sight of work in that rock-hard, west Texas ground. Pierce himself was down in the well, along with another fellow. A third man stood atop the well, hoisting up buckets of dirt and tossing it aside.

Pierce wiped at the mixture of dirt and sweat on his forehead and looked up at me. "Help slide that ladder down here," he said, "and I'll climb out."

I did, and Pierce came up from the well. He was dirty from head to foot. "Been working on that well for a month. Thought maybe the rain would have softened the ground, but it didn't."

"I swear to God, Hawkins, sometimes I get a mind to sell everything I own and take off for the east. Maybe buy myself a little farm and spend the rest of my days growing corn. That or drive my cattle west and start over. I hear there's some fine, cool, mountain valleys over to New Mexico where the grass grows saddle-high."

"What made you settle this area, anyway, Mr. Pierce? Ain't much water, and you got to look hard to find two blades of grass growing together. No, sir, was I going to start my own ranch, it wouldn't be here."

Pierce walked to a water trough nearly two hundred yards from the house, and I followed along. He dipped his head into the murky water and came out shaking the water off like a dog. "If I don't strike water up closer to the house, I may have to move," he said. "Used to have a well over on the east side, but she up and went dry."

He ran fingers through his wet hair, put on his hat. "It's easy enough to wonder why a man would settle here," he said. "Sometimes I wonder myself. But after the war there wasn't enough cash money in this whole state to weigh down a man's pocket.

"But we had cattle. Millions of cattle. Got so a cow and a calf was worth ten dollars, and you could buy anything you wanted using a pair like that in place of money.

"That aside, Hawkins, this is good country. We had Comanche to deal with. Bandits and such crossed the border now and again. But at least a man knew who his enemies were. Can't always say that about your friends.

"And there's grass and water a-plenty for one ranch. Maybe two or three. Guess I never looked ahead to a time when squatters would be a problem.

"And if that ain't enough, I got two sons and a wife buried on that hill back yonder. This is my country, Hawkins. I bought it with blood and I won't sell it for less."

As we walked back toward the house, I told him I'd

taken on the job of foreman for the Reverse Box E. Pierce never slowed his stride. "Then why are you here?"

"To strike a bargain. Beth Alison ain't looking to put you out of business, but she wants the grass on her range for her own cattle. She's agreed to leave a way or two open so your cattle can get to the Pecos."

"Well, ain't that sweet of her! Hawkins, you know as much about cattle as I do. The water is important, but a longhorn can walk all day to reach it, if needs be.

"Thing is, every step they take cuts down on the weight, and that takes money out of my pocket. My cattle need to get to the river, but they need good grass along the way."

"Beth holds title to most of that land, and the grass on it."

Pierce laughed. "You know how she came to have title, Hawkins?"

"Filed on it, I reckon."

"Jim Alison filed on it. He came along only a few years after I did, and fought his share of Indians and outlaws. We were friends, and if he'd been as ambitious as I was, Mrs. Alison would be driving a hell of a lot more cattle than she is.

"We both filed on land, thinking to keep others out, but we started too late. Jim let my cattle on his grass, and I let his cattle on mine. That's how we intended it.

"Then he went off and married that city woman. When he was killed she took over, and all of a sudden it's her grass. Jim never intended it that way, and well she knows it."

"Times are changing, Mr. Pierce. I reckon it won't be long before there ain't an acre of land in the state that somebody don't hold claim to. I imagine it'll all be fenced in, to boot.

"We got to work things out, Mr. Pierce. We'll let your cattle through to water, but not to the grass. This range is overstocked, and if something isn't done, it'll be ruined for cattle."

We reached the house and Pierce went in. He led the way into the kitchen and poured us both a cup of coffee at a heavy table. He lit a cigar and offered me one, but I rolled a cigarette instead. The coffee wasn't fresh, but it was strong.

"Hawkins," he said, "I can't do it. If it was just me an' Mrs. Alison fighting for grass, maybe we could work it out. But we ain't the only ones. There must be six, maybe eight small ranches about, all trying to run cattle on the same range.

"My boys chase off one squatter, and two others take his place. They come in here with nothing but a horse, a wife, a bunch of kids, and a branding iron. They build a dirt-roofed shack and go to branding everything in sight.

"You're right about the range getting overstocked, but it always has been. Used to be that when the cattle chewed things down, why, they'd just leave for new range. Then me an' Alison started ranching, and when the cattle built up we'd drive a bunch to market.

"Now the squatters all have a brand, and most of 'em don't know nothing about longhorn cattle, or about ranching. So it's come down to who'll make it through, and who won't. I plan to be here when the others are long gone and forgotten."

He flicked ash from his cigar, stood up, and looked out the window. "I like this country, Hawkins. It may be bone dry, covered with prickly pear, mesquite thickets, and rattlesnakes, but it's almighty pretty."

He turned back to me. "Tell Mrs. Alison to pull down her wire, and we'll work something out. If she ain't started by next Monday, I'll tell Brice Campbell to pull it down for her."

"If he tries, there'll be blood on the land."

"It won't be the first, and likely not the last. I've gone as far as I can go, Hawkins. I'd work with Mrs. Alison if I could, but she's putting up wire, and if I let her get by with it, every squatter for a hundred miles around will be doing the same.

"I can't do it, Hawkins. I can't. Tell her to start pulling down wire by Monday. That's my final say."

I nodded, drank the last swig of bitter coffee in my cup. A few grounds came with the coffee. Standing up, I rolled another cigarette, lit it. "I'll tell her, Mr. Pierce, but I know what her answer'll be."

Going outside, I climbed into the saddle and rode back to Comanche Creek. The rain started up again, though not hard. But by the time I reached Comanche Creek I was soaked through and shaking like a leaf in the wind.

Stopping in at the saloon, I had a whiskey to get my blood moving again. Brice Campbell and half a dozen Rocking M hands came in, Johnny Stevens with them. We had a drink together, and I told them pretty much the same thing I'd told Neal Pierce.

Brice swore. "Guess that's it, then. Well, Hawkins, here's to straight shooting."

We both drank. Johnny didn't join in. "It don't seem right," he said. "I don't want to shoot at you, Ben."

"Can't say I want to shoot at you, Johnny. But we'll both do what we have to."

"I reckon. But it still don't seem right."

Ruby wasn't about, so I went out and rode off toward the Reverse Box E without saying goodbye. Neal Pierce wasn't the kind to say something unless he meant it, and Beth Alison wasn't the kind to back down unless she had to. Come Monday they were going to butt heads, and a lot of cowboys were going to be caught in the middle.

And one of those cowboys was going to be me. I didn't like anything about it. But hell, neither did anybody else, Neal Pierce and Beth Alison included.

It didn't matter. Like it or not, it came down to who was

going to be left standing. If Beth Alison could hold off Pierce and fence in her land, she'd be the boss of the range, and squatters would cut Neal Pierce down to nothing.

On the other hand, if Neal Pierce could tear down the wire and drive Beth Alison out, the squatters would be afraid to move in. They'd stay at the edge of the range, and Pierce would claim title from the Pecos north.

And try as I might, I couldn't for the life of me figure out who was right and who was wrong. Or even if it mattered.

CHAPTER 9

AFTER TELLING BETH about the talk I'd had with Neal Pierce, I set about preparing the Reverse Box E for war. Three hands quit when I laid it all out for them. Delmar Cross, Vernon Brown, Lonnie Miller, Don Weaver, and Bob Parker all decided to stick.

On Saturday I hired two more men, Travis Ward and Jim McKay, bringing the number of men riding for the Reverse Box E to seven, not counting Billy or me. It wasn't enough. We needed twice as many men, maybe more. But it looked like the Reverse Box E was on the losing side, and not many were willing to sign on.

Beth didn't have a lot of fence strung yet, not by Texas standards. Taken altogether, it worked out to something like four or five miles of wire. That left near thirty to forty miles of wire to put up, if she wanted to do things right.

Barbed wire and fence posts, both of which had to be bought and shipped in, cost money. Beth had sold a small herd of prime steers near a year earlier, and the take was enough to cover most of what she needed. Fact was, she already had a barn full of wire and posts, but we'd need more. A lot more.

If the Rocking M let us string it. That was the thing. One man with a pair of wire cutters could tear up as much fence in a night as we could put up in two weeks. That meant we'd have to have a couple of men riding the fence day and night, and we were already shorthanded.

It seemed best to alternate the work, so I gave Bob Parker and Travis Ward shotguns, and had them start off the nightriding. Come Monday morning, the rest of us loaded a wagon with fence posts and went to work planting them in the ground.

My idea was to plant a mile or so of posts, then stretch wire along them. Bob and Travis had ridden fence all night, so I left them back at the bunkhouse. I had Don Weaver stay back with Beth and Billy in case of trouble there; that left five of us to put in the posts.

The rain had softened the ground a bit, but slamming that posthole digger into it was still work, and most cowboys frown on anything that can't be done on horseback. I'd hired good men, though, and all tackled the digging without complaint. Three of us dug at once, spacing the holes fifty feet apart.

Wherever possible, I had the two men not working take rifles and stake out a spot on high ground. That way we had two men ready in case of attack, and by trading off, it gave us all a chance to rest.

Noon came and we broke for coffee and a bite to eat. The day was windy and cold, though it hadn't rained since Saturday. Vernon Brown built a small fire in the shelter of a wash and put on coffee. We made do with cold beef and biscuits, but ate like it was the finest food we'd ever put teeth to.

After eating we went back to digging holes. Along about three I took a turn standing guard with Jim McKay. We were sitting on a rise of ground seventy-five yards back from the line of posts, talking to each other but watching the skyline for signs of trouble. We both had Winchester repeating rifles, and those things held fourteen shots apiece.

Even at that, we almost missed the trouble when it came. The Rocking M men came in two bunches of eight or ten men each, charging in from a long wash to the east and from behind a rise of ground to the north. They came fast, and they came firing. If McKay and I hadn't been setting back with rifles, they'd have had us cold.

Miller, Brown, and Cross all broke for the wagon, bullets kicking up dirt all around their feet. Then we cut loose and caught the Rocking M riders by surprise.

Now, I'm not worth much with a wheel gun, but I could more than hold my own with a rifle. The Rocking M riders were no more than a hundred and fifty yards out and closing fast when we started firing.

My first shot took a rider out of the saddle, and my second cartwheeled a horse. We had them dead to rights, and I fired as fast as I could work the lever. A man grabbed his arm and almost fell before catching his balance. Another grabbed at his stomach, and even from the distance, I heard the whump of the bullet striking his gut.

McKay was firing at the other bunch, but I let him be, never even looking to see if he needed help. My rifle clicked on empty and I brought it down to reload. Only there was nothing left to shoot at.

The Rocking M men broke and ran, and in less than a minute were out of range. They left three men on the grass from the bunch I'd been shooting at, and two others from the men on McKay's side.

When we were sure they'd gone, we walked down and looked things over. The two men McKay shot were dead. One of the men I'd shot was dead, his eyes open and sightless, looking up at the gray sky that was the last thing he ever saw. Another of the men was winged, a bullet creasing his forehead and dazing him.

The third man had a bullet an inch above his navel, dead center. It came out his back, leaving a wicked hole. I knelt down beside him and examined the wound. It didn't take more than a glance to know there wasn't a thing anybody could do. I told him as much.

He was clutching at his stomach, and sweat stood out on his forehead in spite of the cool day. "It hurts," he said. "God, it *hurts*!"

"I 'spect so. You want whiskey?"

He nodded, spoke through gritted teeth. "Anything."

I fetched a bottle from the wagon and helped him drink all he could take. It seemed to ease the pain some. "Never figured it like this," he said. Then he closed his eyes, breathed ragged for a minute, and died with me holding his head up off the ground. Easing his head down, I took a long pull from the whiskey myself. I'd seen a lot of men and boys die during the war, but I never had gotten used to it.

Lonnie Miller was standing nearby, his face white as a ghost. "I never saw a man killed before," he said.

I tossed him the whiskey. "It won't help much," I said, "but it'll take the edge off."

McKay had taken the Colt from the wounded Rocking M rider and had a rifle pointed at his belly. "You go back and tell Mr. Pierce it didn't work," I said. "Tell him to come along next time, if he's got the guts."

"He won't play that game, and you know it," the man said. "And if Brice Campbell had been along this time, it'd be me holding a rifle on your belly."

"Brice wasn't along?"

"You didn't see him, did you?"

"Where was he?"

The man spat on the ground. I backhanded him across the mouth, splitting his lip wide open. "Mister," I said, "I can shoot you right here and no one would ever know. Best thing you can do is answer my questions. Now where was Campbell?"

He didn't like it, but he answered. "He got throwed from a horse day before yesterday. He'll be all right, but he hurt his back some."

"Why'd he send you on without him?"

"Mr. Pierce's idee. He figured we could ride right through you all. Reckon he was wrong."

"I reckon. You'd best get to walking. It's a long way to the Rocking M."

"Walking? You ain't gonna make me *walk!* Hell, it must be twenty miles."

"Close to it. So, like I said, you'd best get to it."

He gave me a sour look, but he turned and walked off, dabbing at his cut lip with the back of his hand. I watched him for a time, then turned back to the men. "We'd best get some graves dug," I said.

We dug the graves, not making them any deeper than necessary, then covered them with rocks. "Might as well call it a day," I said. "We've planted enough fence posts, and enough men, for one day."

By the time we rolled back up to the bunkhouse, I was in a foul mood. Taking on the Rocking M just wasn't going to work, not the way we were going about it. We were lucky today, but it was the kind of luck you know won't last.

Had Brice Campbell planned the attack, and had he been along to see it went off as planned, it would have been a different story, and well I knew it. Brice wasn't the kind to go charging blindly into a setup. He'd have known we had two men staking out the high ground with rifles, and he'd have found a way around it.

And if push came to shove, there was nothing in Brice Campbell's rule book that said he had to play fair. He was reputed to be a crack shot with a rifle and to have killed more than a few men from ambush. He wouldn't hesitate to kill a few more, and there was nothing harder to deal with than a man with a rifle who didn't care what his target was. And Brice wouldn't give a damn.

If we were going to have a chance, even a small chance, we had to have more men. At least half a dozen more. With only eight men we could fight, or we could work. We couldn't do both. With another half dozen men, there was a chance of holding off the Rocking M and still keeping the ranch from going to hell.

Comanche Creek was too small a town to pick up new hands, so that was out. In fact, the closest place where I might find some men was San Angelo, seventy-five miles or so to the north, and even that was stretching things. But a stretch or not, it was the only hope we had.

After washing off some off the grime, I went up to see Beth. She was in with Billy. Doc Hall had changed the bandage on Billy's leg the day before and said it was healing fine. Billy didn't seem to think so.

Beth had brought him a tray of food, and he was picking at it when I came in. " 'Bout time you got your appetite back," I said. "You were getting so thin you couldn't cast a shadow."

"Beth said she wouldn't leave until I ate," he said. "She's stubborn as a mule."

"You'd better believe it," Beth said. "Keep it in mind next time you decide not to eat."

I grinned. "How ya doing, Billy?"

Billy shook his head. "It hurts, Ben, and it itches something fierce."

"I'd think it would."

"Naw, I don't mean where it's cut, Ben. I mean my foot hurts. And sometimes it itches so much between my toes that it near drives me loco."

"I've heard such things, Billy. Don't know what causes it. Sounds mighty odd."

"I'd never have believed it," Billy said. "But it's my foot, and I can feel it. I know it ain't there, Ben, but I can still feel it.

"Sometimes I'll forget my foot ain't there, and I'll go to wiggle my toes without thinking. And they move, Ben. I know they're gone, but they move."

Sitting there in the bedroom, I told Beth and Billy about the attack. "I'm going to ride up to San Angelo," I said. "We need more men, and a cook, can I find one. Don't know where else to look for them."

"Will you be gone long?" Beth asked.

"No tellin'. A week, anyway. Maybe a bit longer. Don't see a help for it.

"Right now we can't string fence proper, we can't keep the herd together, and we can't put up a proper fight. There hasn't been much of a rustler problem hereabouts, but you can bet that won't last.

"Once word of a range war spreads, every rustler who hears it'll come looking for easy pickings. There's been more than one rancher who won a range war, then went broke because rustlers picked him apart."

"What can we do about it?"

"Like I said, we got to hire more men. And if the chance comes, we might drive as many cattle as possible into the breaks north of here. They'll be hell to gather again, but rustlers would have the same trouble."

Beth leaned back and her eyes were worried. "Maybe I'm wrong, Ben. Maybe I should forget about fencing in my grass. If I stopped, Pierce wouldn't have reason to bother us."

"Maybe. But Pierce was right about one thing, Beth. There's too many ranches running cattle on this range. They're mostly small ranches, but put together they mount up.

"If you want it plain, I think you'd have been better off not to have started fencing in the grass. But you did start, and now you got to finish it. If you don't, this ranch won't last a year."

"Sometimes I don't care, Ben. But this ranch is all I have left, and Jim wanted it to amount to something. So I'll fight for it, but I wish there was another way. A way to turn this ranch into something without more bloodshed."

"All we're doing is defending ourselves, Beth. It's the Rocking M doing the attacking. I can see why Pierce wants to stop wire from going up, but in the end, it has to.

"I ain't so smart as some, I guess, but I been all over this state, and drove cattle north ever since the war. We don't string wire, we'll find ourselves outside of somebody else's, just like Pierce."

"I suppose so. When are you leaving for San Angelo?"

"Tonight. I'd as soon nobody from the Rocking M knows I'm gone. Might be I can sneak off an' no one'll be the wiser."

Beth nodded. "You'll need some money."

She stood up and left the bedroom. Billy hitched himself up in bed. "The doc said I could start using crutches in another couple of days, and start on a wooden leg in two weeks or thereabouts. Never thought I'd look forward to a wooden leg, but it sure sounds better than lying in this bed day in and day out."

"I reckon that'd drive me crazy, sure enough."

"You think I'll be able to ride a horse, Ben? Or work cattle?"

"Hell, look around, Billy. Some of the best cowboys I ever knew lost a leg or even an arm during the war."

"If you say so, Ben."

"I do."

Beth came back and handed me five hundred dollars in cash. "I'm not broke yet," she said, "but it wouldn't hurt to sell a few head. Any chance of rounding up a hundred steers?"

"If I can hire more men. Right now it'd be risky."

"Hire whoever you can, Ben. Promise them whatever pay it takes, but hire some men."

"I'll do my best. Keep the men close while I'm gone. No tellin' what Pierce will try next."

"You'll want to eat before you leave. I'll get started on supper."

Beth went to the kitchen, and I stood up. "Anything I can do for you before I leave, Billy?"

"How about slippin' a swig or two of whiskey in here? Beth said I wasn't strong enough yet, but I ain't had a drink since I got shot. Reckon that's half my trouble."

"Beth'll have my hide, but I'll see what I can do."

There was a room off to the west side of the house with a cast iron tub in it, and I heated water, then took a bath. By the time I'd shaved, dressed, and emptied the tub, Beth had supper done.

I had the boys come up from the bunkhouse and eat with us, wanting to lay out the work and such I wanted done while I was gone. Mostly I told them to take turns riding the fence in pairs, and to stay close to the house otherwise.

Delmar Cross was a long-legged, bony man from up Missouri way. He swallowed a mouthful of pinto beans, looked from Beth to me. "We got a bunch of cattle scattered between the fence line and the Pecos," he said. "You want we should start pushing them north?"

I thought for a minute. "So long as two of you stay here at all times, go ahead. And you might cut out any likely-looking steers. Might be we'll send some up the trail if the chance comes."

Standing up, I went to the stove and poured myself another cup of coffee. "You boys go ahead and finish your meal," I said. "I'll be leaving soon as it's dark, so I'd best go cut myself a fresh mount."

Detouring through the den, I dug through the liquor cabinet and found a bottle of whiskey no more than a quarter full. Slipping it into my pocket, I went in and gave it to Billy. He smiled. "Thanks, Ben."

"Just don't tell Beth where it came from," I said. "Though I reckon she won't stay mad for a week."

Then, coffee in hand, I went outside and down to the corral. After rolling a smoke and finishing my coffee, I looked over the horses. A knotheaded roan with an evil eye and spur-scarred flanks trotted right up to the fence and snorted.

"You look up to a long ride," I said.

He snorted again, and I went for a rope. He shied some

when I stepped inside the corral, but settled down when the loop dropped over his head. I had a double-rigged saddle, and he didn't seem to mind wearing it, but when I climbed aboard he let me know where those spur scars came from.

It was nip and tuck there for a while, but once he knew I could ride a bit, he eased off and walked out of there gentle as a plow horse. I tied my bedroll behind the saddle, took a few supplies from the cellar, and went up to let Beth and the others know I was leaving.

That done, I pointed the roan north and set off at a trot. I figured to ride most of the night and a good part of the morning. Once well away, I could ride by day and sleep by night, but there at the start I didn't know who might be watching, or what Pierce might try if he knew I was gone.

CHAPTER 10

I RODE STRAIGHT through the night, avoiding the prickly pear and the mesquite thickets whenever possible. There was a half-moon that gave off a good bit of light, but it was behind clouds most of the time.

The going was slow, but I didn't really care. All I wanted was to be well away by morning. It was a cold, blustery night, and I was tempted to stop and build a fire: I couldn't think of anything that would taste better than a cup of hot coffee.

I thought about it for a time, decided against it. Come morning, if I was far enough north of the range where any Rocking M riders might be, there'd be time for a fire and coffee. So, for the rest of the night I shivered in the saddle and pushed north.

In the dim light of early dawn I saw a jackrabbit dart between two clumps of mesquite, a coyote hot on its tail. The day brightened gradually, and along about ten in the morning I found a trickle of water that would likely join in with the Devil's River if it didn't peter out beforehand.

I made camp there, building a small fire and putting on coffee. I hadn't brought along much in the way of food, but I did have salt pork, coffee, and two cans of peaches. All I had in the way of utensils were a small, cast iron skillet and a coffeepot, but anything more would have been a waste.

After putting on the coffee, I sliced the salt pork into the skillet, then opened a can of the peaches with my knife. I've always had a love for peaches, and that can went down my throat in nothing flat. I drank the juice, flattened out the can with my heel, then tossed it in the fire to burn off the label and any peach juice I'd missed.

Come time to leave, I'd bury it along with the ashes from the fire. No sense in making it easy for anybody else to know where I'd stopped, should someone be trailing me. I'd no real reason to think anybody had seen me slip away from the Reverse Box E or that I'd be followed if I was seen. But leaving as little sign as possible was a matter of habit.

After eating, I rode a mile west, made a wide circle, and set up a new camp where I could see my backtrail. It was getting colder, but this time I did without a fire. Undoing my bedroll, I crawled between the blankets and went to sleep, thinking to get just enough in to let me make it through till night.

I slept a solid three hours, waking up only when the roan snorted. First thing I did after getting awake was to spend ten minutes watching back the way I came. I saw nothing. The roan stared back that way, his eyes locked and his nostrils flaring, but I still saw nothing.

The roan hadn't been gelded yet and was still more than half wild and all mustang. He wouldn't do in a proper re-muda; most cowboys wouldn't touch a stallion or a mare because they were too likely to act up. Most times I felt the same way, but on a trip like this a stallion was a fine thing.

A half-wild mustang stallion can smell another horse a godalmighty long ways off, and he generally thinks every mare ought to be his, and every stallion is an enemy. So he'll let you know quick if scent from another horse drifts to his nostrils.

That's how he was acting now, like he'd caught wind of another horse, but I saw nothing. Well, there were still wild mustangs roving about, and like as not, it was something like that he'd smelled. Breaking camp, I saddled the roan and started north, one eye still on my backtrail.

That roan was a knowing horse, and my eyes were open as well, but it didn't do either of us a damn bit of good.

Judging by the way the sun had slid down the sky, it happened along about four o'clock. We were trotting along through a stretch of wide-open country, and I still hadn't seen a trace of anyone all day. Suddenly that roan tossed his head and broke stride. Right at that moment I felt and heard a bullet snap past my head.

The boom of a heavy rifle followed a second later, and I kicked the rowels of my spurs in deep; the roan jumped ahead like he'd been shot out of a gun. I felt the bullet strike him, and he stumbled, caught his balance, and ran faster than ever.

A bullet kicked up dirt ahead of us, then another slammed into my leg. Two more shots followed, but where the bullets went, I had no idea. We came to what looked like an old buffalo wallow, and as we did, the roan collapsed.

I kicked loose as he went down, but I still hit hard. We both came to rest inside the wallow, and for a minute there my head was full of fog. When it cleared, I grabbed my rifle from the saddle and hunkered down behind the roan for cover.

He was still breathing, but blood and foam came from his nostrils with every breath, which meant he was lung shot for sure. I reached down for my Colt, thinking to put him out of his misery. The Colt was gone, the holster ripped wide open.

The bullet I'd thought caught my leg had struck my Colt instead. I put a rifle bullet through the roan's head, then eased back and tried to see how bad I was hurt. There was no blood, but my leg throbbed right where the Colt had been, and I reckoned I was bruised some.

For a time I stayed where I was, trying to decide what to do. I'd been too busy getting the hell away from there to pinpoint exactly where the shots came from, but I knew it had to be somewhere along a rise of ground to the west.

It had been a heavy rifle, from the sound of it. Maybe a .45-90 Sharps. And there was quite a delay between the time the bullets struck and the time the sound of the shot reached my ears. That meant the shooter was at least four hundred yards off, maybe more.

That first bullet would've taken me right out of the saddle if the roan hadn't tossed his head and broke his stride when he did. It made me feel cussed ornery to lose him. I hadn't ridden him long, but he was a fine horse, and somebody owed me.

Collecting looked to be a problem. The country was mostly wide open and getting over to that rise of ground was sure suicide. So I lay right where I was, taking a sip of water now and again, waiting for dark.

Along about the time the sun was sliding out of sight, I saw a horse and rider go cutting out due south. I watched until they were out of sight, then sat up and rolled a cigarette. Lighting it, I took a couple of drags, then went to walking along my backtrail.

I found my Colt, but the bullet that tore it from the holster had smashed it beyond repair. Just before full darkness settled in, I found the spot where the bushwhacker had been. From the looks of things, he hadn't been there for more than a few minutes when I came along, and that meant he'd likely been following me and had circled around to get ahead once he saw where I was headed.

He'd picked up the brass from the rounds he'd fired, which meant he was a coolheaded, thinking man. And while he'd ridden off to the south, that's what a thinking man would do if he wanted me to believe he'd given up.

Might be he wouldn't try the same thing twice, and might be he would. With me on foot, it wouldn't be hard for him to circle around and set up a second ambush. Trouble was, I couldn't do much about it.

Except maybe to not go ahead in a straight line. Going back to the buffalo wallow, I stripped saddle and gear from the roan, and loaded down under the weight, I started off toward the northwest.

I walked that way maybe two hours, then abruptly turned and walked due east for another hour. There I stopped and rested awhile, listening to the sounds of the night. I was tired, sleepy, and wanted nothing so much as a chance to crawl into my blankets and sleep a solid eight hours. But not until I found the right spot.

After a rest, I started north again, and two hours later I saw the glow of a dying campfire two hundred yards ahead. Not being a complete damn fool, I stopped right where I was to look things over.

It was already well into the night, and the folks around the campfire were long since asleep. I didn't see a guard, but the fire was so low I couldn't see much of anything, truth be known.

A horse stomped the ground and neighed softly, the sound seeming close by in the stillness of the night. After easing everything I was carrying to the ground except the Winchester, I moved closer to the camp, taking my time.

There wasn't much of a breeze, but I circled around and put what there was at my face, not wanting the horses to get wind of me. Only when I was much closer to the camp did I see the wagon. It had a canvas top and another piece of canvas slung beneath to carry such things as firewood or buffalo chips, though it was getting easier to find a chicken with teeth than a buffalo.

The camp looked normal enough, though there was a shape in the darkness not far from the nearly dead fire that I couldn't make out. I wasn't more than fifteen or twenty yards from the edge of camp before I realized what the shape was. It was a rocking chair, sitting there pretty as you please.

Three blanket-covered shapes lay about the fire, and depending on how the wagon was loaded, there might have been another person or two inside. An iron kettle hung on a swivel pole so it could be swung over the fire to heat, or swiveled away so as not to burn the food. A large coffeepot sat near the kettle.

The horse I'd heard proved to be the only one there, and it was a plow horse. Four big oxen were used to pull the wagon, and that made good sense. Oxen are a good deal slower than horses, but stronger and steadier. On a long haul, oxen will still be going strong after a team of horses has worn out.

Rifle still close at hand, I shouted out a loud hello to the camp. It took three tries before a man stirred and sat up. "Who's out there?"

"Name's Ben Hawkins. Is it all right to come on in?"

"Come ahead."

The man stood up and threw several sticks of mesquite onto the fire. It caught and flared up pretty, throwing light over a good-sized area. Walking into camp, I squatted near the fire, held my hands out to it.

"Got a dead horse several miles back," I said. "I was hoping you'd have a spare."

"No, sir. Just that old mare, and she's never seen a saddle. My name's Jacob Priddy."

"Pleased to know you. Don't suppose there's anything left in that kettle? It's been a spell since I ate."

"White beans and ham. You're welcome to it."

He swung the kettle back over the fire to heat, then took the coffeepot and filled it from a water barrel strapped to the wagon. Jacob Priddy was a man who looked to be somewhere in his thirties. He was tall, but had the stooped shoulders of a man who'd spent his life behind a plow.

As he was carrying the coffeepot back to the fire, another shape stirred and sat up. I saw it was a boy, no more than twelve. "What's going on, Pa? It ain't morning yet, is it?"

"Long ways from it. You go on back to sleep."

We sat and talked low while the beans heated and the coffee brewed. "How'd your horse come to die?" Priddy asked. "Snakebite?"

"No, sir. Ain't many snakes about this time of year. Mostly they're hibernating, and those you do see are sluggish. Somebody shot my horse from under me."

"You don't know who?"

I shrugged. "Got ideas, but that's all. This is still a dangerous country. I never saw him, so there's no telling for certain sure."

"Where you headed?"

"San Angelo. What about you folks?"

"New Mexico. My brother's been out there near five years. He's got his own ranch, and said if we'd come out it'd be share and share alike."

"That was fine of him."

"Yep, but that's Samuel. We owned a spot of ground back in Indiana, but it never was enough to amount to nothing. Our folks been dead near ten years, and the kids didn't have nothing to look forward to but hard work and no money.

"Might be I made the wrong choice, but we all agreed to come."

"Why come so far south? Seems you've gone a long piece out of your way."

"My wife's sister and mother both live over to Austin. Karen wouldn't hear of coming south without seeing them, even if it did mean going four or five hundred miles out of our way.

"Reckon it's a good thing I listened to her, though. We started off in an old farm wagon pulled by two horses. Karen's brother-in-law took one look at 'em and said they wouldn't do. He up and gave us that wagon and the oxen."

I walked out then to get my saddle and other things, and when I come back the food was hot and the coffee ready. I ate, drank two cups of coffee, then smoked a cigarette. That done, I spread my bedroll over out of the way and went to sleep.

CHAPTER 11

IT WAS THE sound of folks moving about that woke me up. My back hurt, but I sat up, coughed, stretched a bit. I was fifteen, twenty yards from the camp, but Jacob Priddy saw me sit up and yelled out a good-morning. I raised a hand, but didn't speak.

"Breakfast'll be ready in a few minutes," he yelled. "You'd best get up and about if'n you want any. This family tends not to leave much."

I cleared my throat. "Yes, sir. Be right there."

Walking off into the brush a piece, I watered a prickly pear, then rolled a cigarette and walked back into camp. I'd only seen three shapes about the fire during the night, but four people were in camp. There was Jacob Priddy and a woman I took to be Karen Priddy. There were also two kids, a boy and a girl, neither more'n thirteen.

Jacob Priddy gave out the names. The boy was Jodie Priddy, and the girl was Lizzie, which I took to be short for Elizabeth.

Mrs. Priddy was a plainly attractive woman, and her face showed little of the wear you generally find on a farm wife. She'd done breakfast up right, making biscuits in a Dutch oven and using real baking powder for leavening.

There was also a pan of gravy and chipped beef to sop the biscuits in, fried bacon, and hot frijoles. Put that together with the pot of hot, strong coffee, and it was the best breakfast I'd had in a coon's age. I said as much.

Karen Priddy smiled. "Thank you, Mr. Hawkins. I assume you aren't married, or you wouldn't think so much of a simple breakfast."

"No, ma'am, I ain't. Don't know as I'd want a woman who'd have me, if you take my meaning. But I've known plenty of men who were hitched, ma'am, and not many ate so well, especially out on the trail."

When breakfast was over, they set about breaking camp, and I lent a hand. When they were ready to go, Jacob held up a minute. "You're welcome to ride along," he said. "I hate to leave you out here without a horse."

"Can't say as I like it, but I been a-foot before, and will be again. I'm bound to come across a ranch sometime today. When I do, I'll buy a horse."

Jacob started the oxen off to the northwest, and hoisting my saddle up, I started toward the northeast. It turned out to be a long day, but an hour shy of dark I spied a couple of riders pushing a small group of cattle just about a quarter mile to the east.

Standing on some high ground, I fired my rifle three times into the air. They pulled up and looked my way, and I waved the rifle to get their attention. Once I was sure they'd seen me, I started walking that way.

It took ten minutes or so to reach them, and they sat and waited. Turned out the two were brothers by the name of Harry and Paul Miller, and they were trying to turn a rawhide spread into a paying ranch. I asked if they had a horse for sale, and they looked at each other.

"Mister," Paul Miller said, "one thing we got for sale is horses. If you got the cash money, that is. Don't look like you got much in the way of trade."

"I got a few dollars, but I can't afford anything fancy."

"We got mustangs," Harry said. "Nothing fancy about 'em, but they'll get you there and bring you back. Give Paul your saddle and hop up here behind me. We'll go take a look."

"What about the cattle?"

"Hell, they won't stray far tonight. And we need money. We can gather this bunch again come morning."

Harry pulled his boot from the stirrup and I used it to hoist myself up behind him. We went off at a trot, coming to an adobe house after thirty minutes of riding. It wasn't much of a place, but it was built tight and would stand up long after its usefulness was gone.

Those boys had a pole corral chock full of mustangs. "They all been saddle broke," Harry said. "We need eight or ten for ourselves, but you pick out one you like and we'll dicker on price."

Going over to the corral, I watched the mustangs prance around. Most cowboys take to horses that are a solid color, and I was no exception. Mustangs come in all shades and combinations of colors you can think of, but most often they're solids. And inside that corral was the prettiest claybank I'd ever laid eyes on.

Now, a claybank is a cross between a sorrel and a dun, and have kind of a yellowish cast. They're almighty pretty, and this one was prancing around as if expecting attention. Shoving my hat back, I rolled a smoke. "Give you thirty dollars for that claybank," I said.

Harry swore and Paul threw his hands up in the air. It was all part of the act, and I knew it. "Thirty dollars?" Paul said. "Hell, the worst horse in there is worth fifty. What about that grulla? That's a hell of a horse. We'll take sixty-five for that'n."

I laughed, ground my cigarette out with the heel of my boot. "I 'spect you would, if somebody was fool enough to pay it. Might go thirty-five on him."

"There ain't no use in talkin', if that's how it's gonna be," Harry said. "We didn't catch and break them horses to give 'em away."

"You got a right to make money," I said, "but not to take a man's life savings for one old horse. Shoot, there ain't a horse here worth more'n forty dollars."

"You feel that way, you can walk on up to San Angelo," Paul said. "Won't put no blisters on my feet."

"Won't put no money in your pocket, either. Tell you what, that claybank does take my fancy. I'll give you forty dollars, cash on the barrelhead."

We went back and forth like that for twenty minutes. Upshot was, I ended paying fifty dollars for the claybank. It seemed I'd come away with a good deal until I had a saddle on him. When I climbed aboard he bowed his back, stood on tiptoe, then went off like a stick of dynamite.

I hung on for thirty seconds, then the claybank went one way and I went the other. My shoulders hit the ground first and the air went out of me. Sitting up, I sucked enough air to keep me alive and looked over toward Harry and Paul. You never saw such innocent faces.

"Thought you-all said they'd been saddle broke?"

"Gentle as lambs," Paul said. "That claybank just wanted to see what kind of rider you might be."

"Suppose you step up there in the saddle and show me how it should be done?"

Paul climbed over the fence, caught up the reins, put a foot in the stirrup, swung the other leg over. The claybank trotted around the corral pretty as you please.

"Well, hell's bells," I said. "Let me back on him."

Paul stepped down and I took his place. This time the claybank let me ride him without offering to buck. Harry was standing at the fence, a big smile on his face. "Don't let Paul fool you, Mister. That claybank always bucks first time he's rode after a spell.

"You give him some work every day, and he ain't so bad. Might be he'll give you a test come a cold mornin', but he's no owlhead. I'd reckon he'd cost you a sight more'n you paid, if you bought him up in San Angelo."

He was right about that, but it wasn't often I'd set astride a horse that bucked like that claybank. I wasn't at at all sure how much jostlin' my old bones could take.

I stayed the night with the Miller boys. Supper was Mexican strawberries and stale corn pone. Breakfast was more of the same. Harry and Paul seemed as poorly put out by the food as I was, and once breakfast was finished we all poured coffee and stepped outside to get some fresh air.

It was a cold morning, threatening rain, and a northwest wind was picking up. A polecat emerged from the mesquite and walked boldly between the house and the corral. Harry sipped at the coffee and watched me as I rolled a smoke. "You got enough of that for a spare?" he asked.

I handed over the makings and he rolled a smoke. Paul did the same, and both sucked the smoke down deep. "Been out of tobacco more'n a week," Harry said. "Thought it didn't bother me until you rolled one."

"You mind some company into San Angelo?" Paul asked. "Now that we got a pocketful of money, there's things we could buy."

"Don't mind the company," I said. "But you oughta know, I had my last horse shot from under me. Can't say the fellow who done it won't try again."

Harry looked at Paul. "That scare you any?"

"Not that I can tell. What about you?"

Harry grinned. "Don't think so. Guess that means we're goin' along."

"Like I said, I'd enjoy the company."

We saddled up after a spell, and that claybank didn't buck worth nothing. We pointed our horses toward San Angelo and went off at a canter. Harry and Paul Miller were typical of the west Texas country. Like as not they hadn't seen more than a year or two of schoolin', and I doubted either had ever read a book.

But they were working men, and come hell or high water, they'd build a paying ranch or go to their graves trying. They wouldn't back down for man nor beast, and anybody picking trouble with them would have to go all the way.

We came into San Angelo of a cold morning . . . be danged if the rain hadn't changed into snow, little icy pieces of snow that stung the skin and made a man duck his head down so's to avoid it. It'd been colder, I'd seen it such, but not for a time.

We tied our horses out of the wind and made for the shelter of an adobe saloon. It was warmer there, nearly hot after being outside. They had an old, potbellied stove in the corner, and a dozen whiskey-drinking men added to the heat of the room.

I bought the first round, and while we sat and drank, I looked about the place. Come winter those cowboys unlucky enough to be out of work fell into two categories: those who'd spent their summer wages and those who'd managed to keep a few dollars in their pocket.

Those who were busted generally spent their days riding the grub line and looking for whatever work they could find. Those with money generally spent their time in saloons, drinking, gambling, and sashaying with the women until they were broke and had to join the others out on the grub line.

And broke or not, a saloon was a place to get warm and sometimes get a free drink or a bowl of day-old beans. Sit in a saloon long enough and sooner or later you'd likely see every cowboy for a hundred miles around, working or not, broke or not.

Me, I needed half a dozen men, could I find them. Not that I was counting on it. I'd settle for three, and count myself lucky if I found four. Finding men willing to step into a range war for fifty dollars a month was a lot to expect. Especially when the Reverse Box E looked to be on the losing side.

It occurred to me that I had two likely prospects sitting around the table with me, and I put the question to them. Harry asked a few questions back, and I laid out the answers, holding back nothing.

Paul scratched his head. "We could use the money," he said. "No two ways about it. Don't know as I like the odds on livin' long enough to spend it."

"That ain't so much my worry," Harry said. "I been shot at before, and likely will be again. Don't know about leaving the ranch for too long a time."

"Comes to that," Paul said, "ain't a hell of a lot we can do before spring roundup, and it won't hurt the cattle to scatter a bit. They walk over hell and gone looking for water and grass anyways.

"We got that remuda to think about, but they got their winter coats long since, and we'd be better off letting them run wild a spell. I druther have them scrounging cottonwood bark than trying to feed 'em ourselves the next couple of months."

Harry took a swig of beer, wiped foam from his mustache. "You for it, then?"

"Like I said, we could use the money. We'd need to swing back by the place and take care of a few things."

"Fine by me," I said. "I'll be in town a couple of days at least. You can wait with me and we'll stop by your place on the way back, or you can go on ahead and I'll swing by on my way home."

"Don't reckon we'll need the supplies we came for," Paul said. "Guess a package of Arbuckle and a few sacks of Bull Durham'll do me. Be best if we go on back to the spread and get things taken care of so's we'll be ready when you come by. That suit you, Harry?"

"Reckon I'll eat a bit, and then run in the mercantile first. I want me a pair of store-bought pants, and maybe a new hat. Then I'll be set to go."

"Do whatever needs doing," I said. "I could use some food and a few more beers myself."

We sat there and drank awhile, then ate what the saloon had to offer. It was lamb, the first I'd sunk teeth in. It was done up Mexican style, with tortillas and molé sauce. Truth is, I'd never thought of lamb as something to eat, though I knew folks did. But it was fine, and the three of us ate until we were stuffed.

Once we were through eating, Harry and Paul went out to spend some of the money I'd paid for the claybank, and I rolled a cigarette. While I was smoking, a man came in who looked like the sort I needed. Big and mean.

He was stocky, with black hair and a cast to his skin like he might be part Mexican. He wore a serape over a canvas jacket, and judging from the worn butt on the .44 Remington in his holster, he appeared to be a man who knew a bit about trouble.

The only way to find out, though, was to go over and talk to him. He sat down at a table, his back to the wall, and waved off the bartender when he yelled out to ask if the man wanted a drink. Picking up my own beer, I walked over to the man's table. "Name's Ben Hawkins," I said. "Mind if I sit down?"

"What for?"

"I work for a spread down south of here, and I'm looking to hire men."

"Cowhands are a dime a dozen this time of year. Why pick on me?"

"We're right in the middle of a war," I said. "The other side's got four or five times as many men, and a hell of a lot more money. Not many want to ride for us."

"What makes you think I do?"

"Nothing. Only you don't look like a virgin . . . or a cowboy, for that matter."

He grinned. "Nope, can't say I'm either. Sit down, Mister Hawkins. If there's a beer in it, I'll at least listen to what you have to say."

I yelled out for two more beers and sat down. "Call me Ben," I said. "Or just Hawkins."

"My name is Chantry Fowler," he said. "Most call me Chan. Give me the story, and we'll see how well I like it."

I gave him the story and he smiled. "A man would have to be a damned fool to sign on with the Reverse Box E," he said. "Or he would have to like taking sides with the underdog."

"Either one of those shoes fit you?"

"Both, I guess. All right, Ben, you've hired yourself a man." He grinned again. "Now that I'm working for you, what are the chances of getting an advance on my wages?"

"How much do you need?"

"Enough for food and a room while we're in town. Maybe a little extra to jingle in my pocket. Say ten dollars?"

I gave him a double eagle. "Make it twenty," I said. "You mightn't have a chance to enjoy yourself after this."

"Pleasure is where you find it," he said. "But I will take advantage."

"Do that. I still need two or three men, but right now I want a bath and a room. If you need me, I'll be at the hotel."

The hotel wasn't much of a place, but they had a tub and I used it, then crawled into bed and slept half the afternoon away, something I hadn't done in a long spell. Well, I'd told Chantry Fowler to take advantage of things, so it figured that I ought to do the same.

It was Harry and Paul Miller who woke me up. Not being able to find me, they'd asked at the hotel and were given my room number. They came up and banged on my door, wanting only to tell me they were pulling out.

I told them I'd be along in three or four days, and we left it at that. Once they were gone, I splashed water on my face and went down to the saloon. I needed to hire more men, but I was already getting edgy. There was no way of telling what was happening back at the Reverse Box E, and it was making me worry a bit.

I'd already hired three men, and while I needed three more, I couldn't wait on them forever. I'd give San Angelo forty-eight hours, and that was it. If I couldn't hire the men I needed by then, I never would. Forty-eight hours, and I'd start south.

CHAPTER 12

THE FORTY-EIGHT HOURS passed, and when they did I had another two men working for me, though one was a cook. His name was Tom Wooten, and he was only twenty-three but had been a cook on two drives to Kansas. After hurting his back on another drive and being unable to take the bouncing of chasing after cattle, he spent his time learning to cook. I had to take his word on how well he'd learned, but we'd all know soon enough.

The other fellow was named Marty Bass. He never gave his age, but looked to be right up there with me, maybe a year or two older. He told a story that matched my own as well, saying he'd been cut loose for the winter. He'd been through the war, though he rode for the north.

Me, I fought for the south, but I was more'n happy to take him on.

Swinging by and picking up the Miller brothers, we rode on south, coming up to the Reverse Box E right about noon. Cold as it was, Billy was sitting in a chair out on the porch, wearing a coat and draped with a heavy blanket. Beth came out and I passed names around, then had the boys go on down to the bunkhouse.

"Jim McKay wanted to talk to you the moment you got back," Beth said. "He says we've been losing some cattle."

"Rustlers?"

"That's what he thinks."

"Figured it to happen. I'll see McKay after I get a bite and a drink. Billy, what are you doing out and about? Didn't figure you to be up so soon."

"Opened my eyes yesterday morning and got out of bed

without thinkin'. Took a step and fell flat on my face. Swear to God, Ben, I clean forgot my leg was gone.

"But I got up and hobbled about the bedroom, and that made me itch to get out. Trying to convince Beth that I was ready took more effort than hopping around on one foot. She finally gave in this morning. Dadgumit, Ben, winter or not, it sure feels good out here."

"I ain't never lost a leg, but I was laid up for near a month one time with a bout of pneumonia. Figured I'd go buggy for certain. Fresh air tastes real good after being laid up like that."

"That happen in the war?"

"Nope. Couple of years after. Along about this time of year, come to think of it. Gives me the willies just recollectin' it."

Beth went back into the house, and after talking to Billy for another minute, I followed her inside. She had coffee on, and fed me to boot.

It was only while putting away the food that Beth told me the bad news. "We lost a man while you were gone, Ben. Delmar Cross was shot."

I looked up from my plate. "What happened?"

"Nobody knows for sure. McKay thinks it was rustlers."

"Or some of Pierce's men acting like rustlers?"

Beth shrugged. "McKay didn't think so, but I suppose he could be wrong."

"How long ago did it happen?"

"McKay found him yesterday afternoon. He wanted to start tracking the killers right away. I told him to hold off until you were back."

"You did right. Anything else happen?"

"Nothing serious. The Rocking M has riders in Comanche Creek all the time now. Just going into town is risking a fight."

"No way around that. Means we'll likely have to go along to another town for supplies. That all?"

"Just about. Somebody got up close one night and fired half a dozen shots at the house, but they didn't do any real damage."

Wiping my mouth, I stood up. "Reckon I'd best go have a word with McKay."

"I'm worried, Ben. I feel like we're sitting on a powder keg with a lit fuse. Sooner or later it's going to blow us all up."

"You mightn't be far wrong," I said. "All we can do is be ready when it does blow."

I went down to the bunkhouse, but Don Weaver was the only one there outside of the new men. He was trying to restitch the sole of a boot and making a poor job of it.

"Never was no hand at this kind of work," he said. "What I need is a new pair of boots, but riding into Comanche Creek ain't healthy these days."

"McKay been around?"

"Said he was going over to those breaks to the northwest. We got a good many cattle stashed back in there, but McKay wants to push 'em across the river."

"That'll leave them wide open for rustlers crossing the border."

"Like as not, but you'll have to talk to him about that. I 'spect he has his reasons."

"Could be. Can I find him, I'll listen to them."

"Shouldn't have no trouble. We pushed near seven hundred head over to those breaks already. McKay'll likely be at the end of the tracks. He's real upset about losing Delmar, and I know dang well he don't want to lose no more cattle."

"Where's the rest of the boys?"

"Here and there. We're stretched thin. Vernon and Lonnie are out riding fence, and I'd guess Bob and Travis are close by the cattle.

"All I know for certain is that I got elected to stick close by the house today."

Telling the new men to settle in and get comfortable with the place, I rode off to the northwest. It didn't take long to find Jim McKay. He told me about finding Delmar.

"Something I didn't tell Mrs. Alison," he said. "Delmar was shot in the back of the head from close up. His hair was burned by the powder flash."

"It don't seem likely anybody could get that close."

"No, sir, it don't. Especially since he was riding herd at the time. Whoever shot Delmar had to be riding a horse, they had to be behind him, and they had to be almighty close."

"There's no way a man on a horse could get close without Delmar knowing it."

"Nope. And no way he'd let somebody he didn't know ride behind him. Delmar was a cautious man."

"So he knew the man who killed him."

"Had to."

I looked out across the broken hills. It was warmer than it had been for weeks, but suddenly the air seemed cold. Or maybe I did.

"It might not have been one of our boys," I said. "Delmar surely knew other folks about?"

"Likely, but why would any of them be out here?"

"Come to steal cattle?"

"Could be. We got some missing. Fifty, sixty head. Drove off southwest after Delmar was killed."

Rolling a smoke, I tried to think. "Beth said you wanted to take off after the rustlers."

"Wish I'd done it, too."

"Think there's still a chance to catch them?"

"Depends on where they drove the cattle, and how hard they're pushing. You thinking of going after them?"

I lit the cigarette. "If the man who killed Delmar is one of ours, I want to know it. You got any idea where the boys were when Delmar was shot?"

McKay took off his hat, ran fingers through his hair.

Then he looked me in the eye. "Been thinking about that since I found Delmar. I can account for Travis and for Don. Travis was with me, and Don was riding the stretch of fence over to the east.

"He brought back a fence stretcher I left out there, so I know he went where he said. He didn't have time to do both. Vernon and Bob were supposed to be rounding up more cattle and pushing them to the breaks, and Lonnie was taking his turn at the ranch, so I reckon he's clear.

"Thing is, Vernon and Bob were riding here and there, hunting through the nooks and crannies for strays, and either of them could've rode over to where Delmar was watching the herd. I hate to think of either of those boys doing something like killing Delmar, but they could've, and that's a fact.

"And for that matter, there's ways of looking at things that could make any of us guilty as sin. Don might have rode out and fetched that fence stretcher the night before and saved it for an alibi. Me an' Travis might be in it together. Well, you get the idea."

"Damn, I was hoping it'd be easy to tell. Reckon it's never easy."

"Don't seem to be."

"Beth said you didn't think it was Rocking M men who did this?"

"I wouldn't put it that strong. Only, why would they bother stealing the cattle? Stampeding them over hell and gone, sure. But driving them away like they done, all neat an' tidy? You tell me?"

"I see your point. Don said you wanted to move the herd across the Pecos. Risky, ain't it?"

"Not if we can spare two men to guard them. There's a box canyon just into the Glass Mountains that's perfect. Two men, or even one good man, could get high up in the rocks with a rifle and keep an army off the cattle."

"A box canyon? I hadn't thought of that. Might be a tough job keeping men out at night."

"You ain't seen the place. The opening is real narrow. Grass is the problem. There's enough to keep the herd going two or three weeks, maybe a month. Then we'd have to move them."

"Don't know as this trouble'll be gone in a month."

"That's the thing, boss. If it ain't over in a reasonable amount of time, Neal Pierce is going to get low on patience. Sooner or later he'll go after the cattle, and I figure those Rocking M boys can do more harm to the herd than a hundred rustlers."

"That makes good sense," I admitted. "All right, we'll push the herd over the river. I hired four more riders and a cook, so it won't take all of us."

"Sounds like you have something else in mind besides moving the herd."

"I do. Who's the best man we have with a rifle?"

"I am. Good with a Colt, too, for that matter."

"Can you track?"

"Pa said I could track a catfish through muddy water. Reckon he wasn't far wrong."

"Then you're the man I want."

"For what?"

"We're going after the cattle. It ain't that losing fifty head will break the ranch, but I want to know who killed Delmar. I don't like the picture you painted."

"You think the Rocking M has a man working for us?"

"Could be. Could also be one of the boys made a deal with some of the rustlers hereabouts. Could be one of the boys hired on just to rustle cattle."

"I hope it wasn't one of our boys killed Delmar. There has to be another answer."

"We'll find it if there is," I said.

"When do we leave?"

"How far is it to that box canyon?"

"Two-day drive, or thereabouts."

"That's too long. Any of the boys know where it is?"

"Sure. Don's been there. So's Lonnie. Why?"

"They can drive the cattle. I want you, me, and maybe one or two of the new boys to head out first thing in the morning. It might be we're already too late, but we won't know less'n we try."

"Even if we catch the rustlers, rooting out the man who killed Delmar might not follow."

I spat, dug out the makings for another smoke. "McKay, you want the truth, I'm playing this whole thing by the seat of my pants. Main reason I'm going after the cattle is because I don't know what else to do. Might be it'll help in finding who shot Delmar, and might be it won't. I just don't know what else to do."

"That's straight talk. Makes me feel better, too."

"How's that?"

McKay smiled. "I been walking in a fog since this thing started. Just makes me feel good to know I ain't in there alone."

"Hell, if me being confused makes you feel good, you ought to be laughing twenty-four hours a day."

Leaving McKay to watch the herd, I rode back to the bunkhouse and started making plans. I was tired, dead dog tired. Not that good, satisfying kind of tired a man gets from doing a day's work, but the kind of tired that comes from trouble.

It was a feeling I'd had all through the war . . . a feeling every soldier had. Trouble and danger wear heavy on a man. And I didn't like it. Given my druthers, I'd have been back in Red Heinlin's smithy, pounding hot iron and working up an honest sweat.

It beats all how a peace-loving man can get himself into a boatload of trouble without half trying.

CHAPTER 13

IT TOOK MORE doing than I'd figured to get things pulled together, so it was late afternoon rather than early morning when we left the Reverse Box E. McKay allowed there were probably five or so in the bunch that took the cattle and killed Delmar, and that was plenty. We couldn't spare enough men to match 'em, but I wanted to come close.

After some thought, it was me, Jim McKay, and the Miller brothers who started along the trail after the cattle. It didn't take long to figure something wasn't quite right. McKay spotted it about the same time I did.

"They're running the cattle," he said. "Pushing them hard and fast."

I nodded. "Might be they just wanted to put some distance between them and us. They likely figured we'd be coming along after them."

"Maybe, but you push cattle like this for too long and some'll start dropping out. The rest will lose a lot of weight."

We followed the trail. The cattle didn't slow much, nor did the men driving them try to conceal their trail in any way. Now, you flat can't hide the trail of fifty cattle and five horses, but you can run them down a stream or over bare rock, and that at least makes things difficult for a tracker. These boys weren't even trying.

Come dark, it didn't seem we'd gained more than a couple of miles on the small herd. Next day was more of the same, though we found where three head of cattle had dropped out with broke legs, and four others from just being plain tired. Still they pushed the remaining cattle hard, but we pushed even harder and made up some ground.

We camped that night near a small water hole in the Glass Mountains. The day came in warm, and even nightfall didn't bring much of a chill. It felt like an early spring was on the way.

We kept the fire small, just big enough to heat up coffee and beans. Harry Miller was sittin' back a piece, sippin' at coffee and smoking a cigarette. After a time he looked up. "Any of you done any thinking about where those boys out there are driving the cattle?"

"Mexico," I said.

"You'd think so, but in case nobody noticed, the trail slid off a bit south today. Not much, but enough to steer away from the border."

A funny look came across McKay's face. "Be damned if you ain't right," he said. "We spent the day pushing so hard I didn't give it no thought. It don't make sense."

I tried to picture the day's travel in my mind. Sure enough, on looking back I could see Harry was right. The trail was sliding south, away from the border.

"Maybe they want to cross farther down," I said. "They sure as hell can't figure to keep them in Texas?"

"That ain't all," Paul said. "They know enough about cattle to keep the bunch running without losing any except them that can't keep up, right?"

"Right."

"But they keep running the cattle anyways. They have to know that bunch won't be worth giving away after a push like this. And hell, if they'd gone straight west those cattle would be over the border by now, and like as not out of reach."

McKay had been chewing on a small stick. He pulled it from his mouth and tossed it in the fire. "They don't give a damn about the cattle," he said. "They're *wanting* us to follow them. Nothing else makes sense."

A chill went down my spine. "How far behind are we? Ten miles, twelve?"

"That's about what I figure," McKay said. "You think we're being led into an ambush?"

"It's a thought," I said. "We'll know tomorrow. Best get some sleep. I want to be in the saddle the moment it's light enough to ride."

"We push too fast," Harry said, "we'll likely run into an ambush without seeing it coming."

"Ambush be damned," I said. "We're being led along like a mule with a carrot, and I want to know why. I want to be in sight of those cattle by noon." If we don't catch those cattle by noon or thereabouts, we're going back. Something smells, and I don't like it."

Harry shoved back his hat. "You think there's an ambush coming?"

"Might be, so ride light and keep your eyes on the skyline tomorrow. I got half a mind to think we won't run into nothing, though."

"Why's that?"

"Just a hunch. We catch those cattle, we'll know for sure."

Harry poured the remains of the coffee on the fire, sending up a plume of steam and smoke. He kicked dirt over the whole mess to make sure it was out, then crawled into his blankets. The rest of us did the same.

It wasn't long before Harry and Paul were snoring fit to wake the dead. I didn't hear nothing coming from McKay, but he acted asleep. Me, I lay there for quite a spell, watching a few clouds sail across the sky. I had a bad feeling right in the pit of my stomach, and nothing I could do made it go away.

Something wasn't right. Whoever took those cattle, they sure weren't looking to get them into Mexico, and they had no intention of selling them, else they would've drove 'em straight over the border. Nope, those cattle were stolen and

Delmar killed just so some of us would follow. I'd bet a new dollar against a worn dime on that.

But why? To lead us into an ambush? Maybe, but it was sure slow in coming. We'd already passed fifty places where an ambush could've been set up, and with luck, we'd catch the cattle by noon. It made no sense. No kind of sense at all.

Except that lump in my belly told me it did make sense, only I wasn't smart enough to figure it out.

Sleep wouldn't come, and after a time I got up and walked down toward the water hole. A half-moon lit the night, letting me see just well enough to watch a scrawny deer dart away from the water as I approached.

Kneeling down, I cupped my hands and drank a bit, then backed off thirty yards and sat down on a rock. I rolled a cigarette, listening to the sounds of the night as I smoked. The answer kept flitting through my mind, going by so fast I couldn't read it. An hour later I was no closer to an answer.

I unbuttoned my pants and watered down a cactus, then went back to camp and crawled into my blanket. Sleep came, but it didn't hurry. Even at that, I was first up and quickly woke the others.

Harry started to put together a fire. I stopped him. "We'll ride hungry today," I said. "Get those broncs saddled and let's go."

We pushed for all our horses were worth. The cattle were a little closer than we'd thought, maybe six miles as the crow flies. We saw them from a mile off, and pulled up short. We covered that last mile almighty slow, guns ready. There was no need.

The cattle were milling about, too tired to do more than walk, and they were alone. McKay rode a quick circle to cut for sign, came back fifteen minutes later.

"Looks like they rode out last night," he said. "There's

no camp about, and the tracks lead off northeast, swinging wide so's to miss us, I reckon."

Paul spat, stood up in the saddle, and rubbed his lower back. "Now why in God's name would they kill a man to get these cattle, run them half to death to get away, then just ride off an' leave 'em?"

That lump in my stomach rose up into my chest. The answer I'd been looking for came out into the open at last. It was about three days late, but it was there. I swore loudly, pulling out a few words I'd forgotten I knew.

"What's wrong with you?" McKay asked.

"I figured it out, that's what. These boys weren't leading us into an ambush. They were leading us away from something."

"Away from what?" McKay asked. Then he answered his own question. "The Reverse Box E. They figured we'd follow the cattle."

"Un-huh. And if the cattle didn't matter enough, they knew Delmar would. That's why he was killed."

"They got us away," Harry said. "But why? They couldn't know how many of us would follow, nor how many would stay behind."

"Likely they had a man watching. We got to get back. If they wanted us away from the ranch, you can bet they had a reason. We got to get back."

"These horses ain't going nowhere without a rest," McKay said. "We'll be afoot within a day if we push. Best give the horses a rest and start off tomorrow."

He was right. I didn't like it, but McKay was right. The horses were done in, and so were we. "All right," I said. "Pierce or Campbell wanted us away, and they did the trick. Whatever they had planned is likely over by now, anyway. No point in killing the horses.

"Spread out and find some water and good graze. We'll give the horses a break and start back tomorrow."

It stunk on ice, but we had no choice. Getting us away

from the ranch, if that had been the plan, had worked. All we could do now was rest the horses and start back when we could. I looked north, a picture of the ranch house forming in my mind.

I'd left eight men back there, not counting Billy. Together they could beat off most any attack. Only, they wouldn't be together much. Except at night. And even then somebody should be on guard.

Yet I knew that's when I would have attacked. Late in the night, maybe right before dawn. Any guard would be sleepy at best, asleep at worst.

It was all guesswork, and I tried to put it out of my mind. Just rest the horses, let 'em get their wind back, then start home. That's all we could do. Worrying and wondering wouldn't help nobody.

We set up camp by a trickle of water, let the horses drink and graze, and put on beans and coffee just like usual. Only it was quiet. Nobody spoke much, and when one of us did have cause to put words out, the answer was usually a grunt.

We started back when we could. With our horses in poor shape we had to take it slow, and it was four days before we came up to the high ground south of the main house. Four days was too long, and I think we all knew we'd be too late.

We were. At least three days late, and maybe more. But even knowing we'd be late, and being certain Pierce wanted as many of us as possible away from the ranch, none of us were ready for what we saw. We topped that high ground and reined in as one man, staring down toward the main house.

For a time we sat there, almost not breathing. Jim McKay broke the silence. His voice was shaky, but came out low and hard. "Damn it to *hell!*" he said.

The ranch house and everything around it, bunkhouse,

barn, tool shed, everything, was gone. Only smoldering piles of ashes and black, charred boards remained.

We sat a quarter mile or so from the house, on higher ground, and had a good view of the surrounding territory. There were no riders in sight. Even so, we slipped our rifles out and jacked cartridges into the chambers.

"You reckon anybody got away?" McKay asked. "Hell, they couldn't have killed everybody, could they?"

"I don't know," I said. "All we can do is go down and look."

Riding ten yards apart, rifles to hand, we started slowly down the slope. We hadn't covered more than half the distance when we saw the first of the bodies.

CHAPTER 14

THE FIRST BODY we came to was that of Vernon Brown. He was lying thirty yards or so from the bunkhouse, and he'd been shot to pieces. Lonnie Miller's body was behind the remains of a wagon, a single hole in the side of his head.

Harry's eyes were cold. "We sat together in the bunkhouse for an hour that first night we got here, just trying to figure if we were kin.

"Got down to it, we allowed we might be cousins, though he didn't know his family well enough to be certain."

"Don't matter," Paul said. "Kin or not, I liked him. Somebody needs to answer for this."

We found two more bodies in what remained of the bunkhouse. There wasn't enough left to recognize, but McKay figured one was Don Weaver, going by a big, silver belt buckle. "Never saw one like it," he said. "That's Don, all right."

The last body was Marty Bass, one of the new men. His face was mostly gone, but two gold teeth remained, and he'd flashed them often enough on the ride back from San Angelo.

"That leaves Chan Fowler, Bob Parker, Tom Wooten, and Travis Ward," McKay said. "And it leaves Miss Alison and Billy."

I nodded. "I'm almost afraid to ride up to the house, but it won't get done no other way."

We rode up to the smoldering ruin of the house without saying a word. There were still hot spots in the ashes, and enough charred boards that hadn't burned completely to make searching a slow, painful process. After nearly an hour of poking about, we found nothing.

"I don't think they're here," Paul said. "You reckon they got away?"

"That, or somebody took them away. McKay, you're the best tracker. See what you can find."

Harry looked around. "Might be he's the best, and might be he ain't. Me and Paul cut our teeth while tracking wild game."

"I believe you," I said. "But give McKay a chance. The fewer tracks we have about, the easier it'll be."

"Can't argue with you there. All right, we'll do it your way."

McKay went to work, doing most of his searching on foot, sometimes on his hands and knees. The rest of us sat and smoked, watching him go this way and that. After twenty-five minutes he stepped into the saddle and rode a couple of circles, going out a bit more each time. Twice we saw him dismount and look at something.

More than an hour passed before he rode back up to us, his face grim. Slipping from the saddle, he dropped onto the cold ground. "Fifteen men came in from the southwest," he said. "Another dozen or so came from yon way. Both groups left their horses some ways back and came ahead on foot.

"The way it looks, they walked right in, torched the house and the bunkhouse, planning to shoot anything that came out to escape the fire. Looks like it worked pretty well, too.

"Only somebody wised up to what was happening and got clear. It was night, had to be, and whoever this fellow was, he put up one heck of a fight. Enough to let Miss Alison, Billy, and somebody else get away."

"How can you tell?" I asked. "The ground looks pretty chewed up to me."

"It is. But see that clump of rock down yonder? Well, sir,

somebody got in there with a rifle and a bunch of ammunition. There's empty brass all over.

"Whoever it was, he was out there in the dark, and the attackers were up here, lit by the fires from the burning buildings. The bodies were carted away, but from the blood I'd say he killed at least three proper, and wounded that many again.

"I found tracks out yonder there where the corral slides off into the high grass. Beth got a horse there, and Billy was with her, though I'm damned if I know how he got that far.

"I can tell you this, too. It looks like Wooten, Fowler, Parker, and Ward all got away, one of them was wounded, and maybe two or three."

"Who do you figure did the shooting out there?"

"Had to be one of the new men," McKay said. "First place, I didn't know the boot print, and second place, neither Ward nor Parker was much with a rifle."

"It was Fowler," I said. "Chan Fowler. Had to be."

"I'd say so," Harry said. "I didn't know him much, but he treated his weapons like another man would a child."

"He struck me as a man who could use a gun," I said. "And I know he wasn't a cowboy."

"Don't overlook Wooten," Paul said. "He was a young, easygoing kind of fellow, but he wore a Colt like a man who could use it."

"Guess we'll know if we can find them," I said. "Any idea which way they went, McKay?"

Jim McKay rolled a cigarette. "Yes, sir. Billy and Miss Alison rode off northwest, over toward the breaks where we keep the cattle.

"Two other fellows headed off almost straight east, going on foot. One of them was leaving blood behind. Another man went off alone, traveling south. Don't know why that'd be, less'n he didn't know the area. Looked like he might have been wounded, too. Wasn't much blood along his trail, but there was some."

"That leaves a man unaccounted for," I said. "Can you tell who the trails belonged to?"

McKay blew smoke. "Not for certain sure. One was Travis, I think. The other two I didn't know. Likely means they belonged to the new men."

"What about Parker?"

"Bob? Now that's a funny thing. Ol' Bob wears a boot the size of a washtub. Hell, a blind man could find his trail."

"So what's funny?"

"Well, his tracks are all about up here around the house, the bunkhouse, the corral, everywhere. Just as fresh as the others. Only, there's no sign of him leaving.

"He didn't leave afoot, or on horseback, unless it was right along the trail of those who burned the place. Be no way to pick him out in that mess."

"You think he followed them?"

McKay stubbed out his cigarette on the ground. "Don't see how he'd have the chance. Look about. Only folks who lived through this were the ones that ran. Somebody did a sight of damage with a rifle, but they ran when the time came.

"I don't know, boss. Might be those Rocking M boys caught Bob and took him along when they left. Don't know what they'd want with him, though."

I rolled a cigarette of my own, trying to think while my fingers went through the motions of building a smoke. My back hurt from all the bouncing about on horseback, my left shoulder was stiff, and there was a pounding right behind my eyes. I smoked the cigarette without saying a word, snubbed it out next to McKay's.

"This is partly my fault, I reckon," I said. "Never figured Neal Pierce to take things this far. Not when he had everything going his way.

"Anyway, we got trouble. Anybody wants to ride away, now's the time. Won't nobody blame you."

"What are you planning?" McKay asked.

I shrugged. "Hell, I don't know. First thing is to find Beth and Billy, if they're still alive. The other boys too, but Beth and Billy first."

"Then what?"

"Then I don't know," I said. "Depends partly on whether we find them alive or dead. But I do know one thing—if I can, I'm going to make Pierce pay for this. Whatever his troubles with the Reverse Box E, he had no call to come in killing and burning like this.

"It's a fool's mission, though. We'd be like a bee stinging a bull. We could get Pierce's attention easy enough, but doing real harm would be tough. So like I said, anybody wants to ride away, you're free."

"Ah, hell," McKay said, "you talk too much. We'd best get moving if we want to find Miss Alison before somebody else does."

Harry and Paul looked at each other. Then Paul grinned. "We ride away now we'll never collect our wages. Reckon we'll stick."

"Just so's you know what you're in for," I said. "Saddle up. We'd best start tracking while there's light to work with."

The tracks of the horse Beth and Billy rode were deep and plain for the first couple of miles. Then they stopped running and started trying to cover their trail. Billy couldn't really do much walking yet, though he'd been whittling on a pegleg when we left to go chasing the stolen cattle. But Beth could walk, and did.

The trail was almost four days old, and in spots it was plain gone. Might be Beth knew something about covering tracks, might be Billy did. Either way, they weren't missing many tricks.

If there was water to be found, they went through it.

When they came to hard rock, they went over it. Then, not long before dark, we found where a group of cattle had been rounded up and pushed along to hide the tracks of the horse.

"That's a fine trick," McKay said. "Used it once or twice my own self."

"What now?" I asked.

"Now we follow the cattle," he said. "Try to spot where the horse breaks away."

"Can you do it?"

"Could on a fresh trail, but this one's getting older by the minute. I don't know, boss. Only thing certain is I can't do it in this light. We'd best find a spot to camp."

Not wanting any of the Rocking M men to track us, we took pains to cover things, and it was coming on dark before we found a spot to camp. I built a fire no bigger than my hat, put on coffee. McKay dug through our things, came up with a small package of beans and two cans of peaches.

"That's about it," he said. "This and the coffee."

"Been thinking about that," I said. "We can always shoot a deer or a steer, so meat's no problem. But we're going to need flour, beans, ammunition, and a few other supplies. Thing is, who's going after them?

"McKay, you're the tracker in the bunch or I'd send you."

"Harry was telling the truth when he said he could track," McKay said. "Him and Paul both spotted things today that I missed."

"That may be, but they don't know the country. No, I 'spect they ought to ride for supplies."

"Either way suits me," Harry said. "Only, like you said, we don't know the country much, so where do we meet up?"

"You can find the river easy enough," McKay said. "Well, about four miles upstream from the ranch there's a bend.

Just north of that is a thick stand of cottonwoods. Big ones. You can't miss them. Take the supplies there and we'll find you."

McKay turned to me. "Thing is, where do we send them? Comanche Creek is suicide for a Reverse Box E rider. Next closest town is what, thirty-five, forty miles?"

"I gave that some thought. Forty miles each way is a long ride, but I don't see no other way."

"I do," Paul said. "We ride into Comanche Creek at high noon, buy what we need, and ride out."

I started to protest, and he cut me off. "You said it was suicide for a Reverse Box E rider?"

"That's what I said. And you two qualify."

"Do we? Hell, ain't none of them seen us, and in case you ain't noticed, our horses are wearing our brand, not yourn. Anybody asks, we never heard of the Reverse Box E."

"That's right," Harry said. "We're just a couple of ranchers headed over to Mexico to buy some horses."

I smiled. "Hell, that just might work. Wouldn't nobody expect Reverse Box E men to come riding in at noon. And it's certain nobody around here would know your brand.

"All right, we'll risk it. We'll meet at the cottonwoods day after tomorrow. If we don't show, give us an extra day, but stay out of sight. Once you show yourselves in Comanche Creek you'll be fair game."

Harry spat. "We won't make a show less'n somebody asks. Might be they'll take a look at our brands and just go along their way. Any way it goes, we'll get the supplies and meet you all."

"Might be we should stop off and get a drink or two, maybe a meal. Won't look right to come into the only town about and ride out thirsty."

"That makes sense," I said. "Go easy though. Have a beer and a bite, then get out of town. No reason to press your luck."

We bedded down not long after making camp, and this time I had no trouble sleeping. Waking up was something else again. The others were already up and about when my eyes opened, and coffee was boiling over the fire.

Being out on the trail had set my spine to hurting again, and sleeping on the hard ground made me stiffer than dry leather. It made me long to be working for Red Heinlin all the more.

Once I had my morning coffee down, I gave Harry enough money to take care of our needs. He and Paul saddled up and rode off east, thinking to hit the road well back from Comanche Creek so it would look like they came in that way should anybody try to backtrack them. I didn't figure they would, but there was no reason to take the chance.

Money was going to be another problem if the trouble lasted much longer. I still had a couple of hundred dollars from the money Beth gave me, but any she had would have went up with the house. More'n likely she had more in the bank somewheres, but I just didn't know.

Likely she did, but it wouldn't help us for a time. It was a safe bet that Rocking M men were scouring the hills even now, looking for those who escaped the fire. And for us. And their orders would be clear . . . shoot on sight. What had been mostly a war of nerves was now a full-blown war of bullets. The few shootings before had been no more than a tuning up, and the whole thing might have been stopped at any time.

Now it was too late.

Tossing the dregs of my coffee onto the fire, I rolled a cigarette and stood up. "We'd best get to tracking," I said. "We've burned enough daylight."

"Guess we have at that," McKay said. "I'll saddle the horses."

CHAPTER 15

THE TRAIL WAS old. Not old enough that McKay couldn't follow, but old enough to give him fits. Beth and Billy were doing their best to hide their tracks, and while McKay was good enough to work through the tricks they pulled, it took time, and that was the one thing we didn't have.

Along about noon we stopped for coffee. McKay was quiet for a time, his thoughts turned inward. "We got to take a chance," he said at last.

"What do you mean?"

"Look at it, boss. We're running four days behind Mrs. Alison and Billy. But that's in time. In distance there's just no telling where they are. . .

"It just depends on what they had in mind. Might be they're holed up within a mile of us, an' might be they're thirty miles away and still pushing. Tracking slow like this, we'll never catch them if they're moving."

I wasn't in the same class as McKay when it came to tracking, but I wasn't all that bad at it. Leastways, I knew enough to see his point. And maybe to see where he was headed.

"So you want to leave the trail? Risky, ain't it?"

"It is. But I'll tell you, boss. This is risky, too. If we don't catch up with them before the Rocking M does, all we'll find will be more bodies."

"What did you have in mind?"

McKay opened his canteen and drank long and deep. Then he sat and stared off to the northwest before answering. "My pa taught me a good bit about tracking," he said. "Later on, a Cherokee who lived not far away added his

121

know-how. Pa and that Cherokee went about things some different, but one thing they both believed.

"Half of tracking is knowing what's in the mind of the thing you're after, be it animal or man. Figure out what they want, and you can sometimes figure out where they're going. So I been asking myself what Mrs. Alison wants. Is she running blind? Does she just want to get as far away as possible? Is she looking for a place to hole up?"

"She won't run any farther than she has to," I said. "She'll go until she believes it's safe, then find a place to rest and think. And she'll be planning some way to get back at the Rocking M."

McKay's eyebrows went up. "Her and a one-legged cowboy? That ain't likely."

"It's certain," I said. "Beth will figure some of us will come looking, and she'll already be planning on where to get more men in case we're dead. Only question is, where will she feel safe?"

McKay pointed to a low rise of hills making up the northwest horizon. "If she wanted distance before holing up, that's where she'd go. See that dip there? That makes up the edge of the Glass Mountains, and the only real water hole out there lies in that dip. Mrs. Alison would know it because now and again we've ridden up that way looking for mustangs.

"If she went through there we might gain a couple of days by leaving the trail and heading for that water hole. But if we ride over there and she ain't been that way, we've lost a day."

"What is that," I asked, "maybe a four-hour ride?"

"About that, if you push hard. Maybe a bit more."

"All right, if I leave now I can get there and have a good look around by dark."

"*You* can get there and have a look around? What am I supposed to do, suck eggs?"

"I'm hungry enough to give it a try. But what I want you

to do is stay on the trail. Like you said, Beth and Billy might be within a mile of us right now. Hell, they might be right around the next bend.

"Nope," I continued, "you stay on the trail as long as you can. If I don't find anything, I'll start back at first light and meet you in that same stand of cottonwoods where Harry and Paul are bringing the supplies."

"What if you don't show, boss?"

"If I'm not there by early afternoon it means I found something. Or something found me. Either way, come a-running."

"You ain't been in this country long yourself."

"Long enough to watch the skyline and steer clear of strange riders."

"That's a start. But you ride easy, boss. We cut several trails today, and I bet they belonged to Rocking M riders. Likely they're all over these hills."

"I'll keep my eyes open. I doubt Pierce has any large groups out. They have to know we're down to slim pickin's when it comes to manpower."

We covered the fire and went our own ways, me hightailing it northwest, and McKay inching straight east along the trail. By pushing hard, I was within half a mile of the water hole with two hours of daylight to spare.

That last half mile took an hour by itself. Thing is, a water hole is like a loadstone, drawing men and animals alike. Especially when it's the only decent water hole for ten miles in any direction. You go riding in blind and there's no telling who or what you'll run into.

Might be there wasn't a thing around the water hole except a thirsty jackrabbit. Might also be there were two dozen Rocking M men sitting around the water hole, drinking coffee, laughing, and waiting for a damn fool like me to come charging in for a drink.

So I took my time, riding wide around the water hole, watching the ground for tracks. There were plenty. Horse tracks, both shod and unshod, cattle tracks, animal tracks of all kinds, and all of them converging on the small water hole. I had to ride a wide circle to make much sense of anything.

An hour before dark I found a trail that sure enough looked like it belonged to the horse Beth and Billy were riding. It was considerably fresher than the trail McKay was following, and after ten minutes on the trail I found a track plain enough to read well. No doubt about it, Beth and Billy had come this way.

The trail was fresher, but still at least a day old, and maybe a bit more. But if I pushed hard, there was a chance of catching up. McKay wouldn't have any trouble finding the trail, especially with my own running beside it, so there was no worry on that score.

My canteen was nearly empty, so I took time to sneak in on the water hole. I was filling the canteen and letting my horse drink his fill when I heard the sound of horses. Me, I was up and heading for cover the moment the sound came to my ears.

We were right at the northwest edge of the Glass Mountains, maybe twenty miles or so north of the Pecos. There was plenty of broken country about, plenty of draws and boulders and hills to hide in. So I leaped into the saddle and went to hide. Only half a mile south I had another notion.

Come morning I had to get back on the trail of Beth and Billy, so I wanted to know who those horses back yonder belonged to. Hiding my claybank in a draw, I took my rifle and my canteen, then started back to the water hole on foot. It was creeping up on dark by the time I arrived.

At fifty yards, I stuck my head over a rock and had a look. Four men milled around the water hole, and one of them I knew for certain. It was Hank Collins. Rocking M men, and no doubt about it.

I was too far away to hear what they were saying, but

after ten minutes or so Hank Collins and one other man rode north and a bit east, going off at a gallop like they had a destination in mind.

The other two men talked a minute, then led their horses behind some boulders thirty yards away. Fifteen minutes later I saw a bit of smoke spring up and knew they were building a fire.

All right, Collins and the other man were riding toward something. What? Meeting someone? Could be. There was no way of knowing. Well, there was one way. Both those boys left to watch the water hole would likely know. And if I asked proper they might be willing to tell me.

And I knew the best time to ask would be about half an hour before dawn, just before they came awake and took up positions to guard the water hole. Slipping away, I walked back to my horse. Moving another half mile away, I built a fire and made coffee.

Food was what I wanted, only I didn't have a thing with me. I'd planned to shoot something worth sinking teeth into, but I'd let it get too late. Besides, risking a shot with so many Rocking M riders about was something I'd only do as a last resort.

Sitting there, I drank most of a pot of coffee and smoked half a dozen cigarettes, then rolled into my blankets and went to sleep.

Hunger and the need to relieve myself of all that coffee woke me up two hours or so before dawn. Just about right. Saddling my claybank, I picked my way back toward the water hole. Two hundred yards away I stopped and tied my reins to a mesquite bush, then went ahead on foot.

Both those boys were still asleep, or so I figured. Only a few red coals still glowed within their fire, and both men were curled in their blankets. Rifle in hand, I stepped into camp just as the first light of dawn swept over the land.

My plan was to prod those boys awake with the muzzle of my rifle, only one of them was playing possum. When I was still ten feet away he suddenly whirled in his blankets, a Remington .44 in his hand. I fired just a split second before he did and his hand jerked, sending his bullet wide.

I fired twice more, slamming his body into the ground. The shots brought the other man awake, and he reached for his Colt, which was lying near at hand. But he was fuddle-brained from sleep and fumbled his grip. Jacking another round into the chamber, I took two quick steps closer.

"You go ahead and try again," I said. "You want to join your friend in the happy hunting grounds it don't make me no nevermind."

He looked at me, at the rifle, then at the body of his partner. He eased away from the Colt. "Who are you?" he asked.

"Name's Ben Hawkins, if that means anything."

"You're foreman of the Reverse Box E."

"I was before you boys burned it to the ground."

He had a worried look on his face, and that I could understand. But how frightened he was I didn't know.

"What do you want with me?" he asked. "I ain't done nothing."

"Were you there when Campbell burned us out?"

He didn't answer. "Mister," I said, "you got a simple choice to make. You can answer my questions and live to see another day, or you can clam up. Do that and I'll put a bullet in your belly and ride off. Your choice."

I dropped the muzzle of the rifle down to the man's stomach and steadied it. He took another look at my face and changed his mind. His hands came out and he started talking. "Whoa, hold on. Ask your questions."

"What happened the night you all burned the ranch?"

He shrugged. "We had those boys in the bunkhouse cold. Or so we thought. It was Campbell ordered us to set things afire while everyone was still asleep. We did.

"Only, somebody got out beforehand. Or they were already out and about. About the time the fires was going good they cut loose with a rifle. I don't know who it was out there, but he was hell on wheels. Every time he pulled the trigger a man went down.

"We hunted cover and shot back, but two or three men made it out of the bunkhouse in the meantime."

"What about Beth Alison and the man with her?"

"Is it all right if I roll a smoke?"

"Do it careful."

He rolled a cigarette and lit it, sucked smoke in deep, blew it out. "I don't know how they got away, and that's the flat truth. One minute they were inside that burning house, and the next they was tearing away on a horse.

"One man stood up to take a shot at them and that fellow out there in the dark put a bullet right through his teeth. The rest of us stayed down.

"Mister Pierce was real upset when we got back that night. He wanted that Alison woman dead."

"How did you all get in so close without being seen?"

He flicked away his cigarette. "Mister, I don't mind talking about that a bit. I may be a lot of things, but I ride for the brand. I got no use for a traitor.

"Fellow name of Parker sold you all out. He said Mrs. Alison was having two men stand guard at night whilst you all were gone, but he'd see to it that he was alone on a given night.

"We came up on foot like he told us. He joined right in when the shooting started, too. Fact is, I know he killed one of your men. Young feller with light hair."

"Where's Parker now?"

"Beats me. Mr. Pierce paid him off, then sent him packing. Reckon he didn't think no more of what Parker did than any of us."

"All right. Hank Collins and the other man. Where were they headed?"

For a minute he looked at me, then decided to answer. "Can't say exactly. Over by Ketchum Mountain."

"Why?"

"Rider came in yesterday morning and said he saw the Alison woman near there, camped near a bit of water some folks call Cholla Creek.

"Campbell was out trying to hunt down you all, so Mr. Pierce sent the four of us. Don't know why exactly, but Collins told me and Wade to stay here and watch the water hole."

"Good enough. Now stand up."

He came to his feet. "Now what?"

"Now start walking. I figure the Rocking M is about thirty miles or so yon way."

"More like thirty-five."

"If you say so. Now you'd best start off. I reckon it'll take some time."

He gave me a dirty look and reached for his boots.

"Leave 'em there," I said.

"What? You don't mean me to walk thirty-five miles barefoot!"

"Mister, I don't care if you walk, run, crawl, or fly. But you leave the boots where they are and get moving. I'm clean out of patience."

He gritted his teeth, but did as he was told. He stopped after thirty feet or so and looked back. "Mister, my name is Quint Toland. You keep it in mind."

"I'll write it down so as not to forget."

"That's a sensible idea," he said. "It's sure certain you'll be hearing it again."

"That's up to you. Tell Neal Pierce and Brice Campbell they'd best hunt cover. From now on I'll be on the hunt."

He sneered. "You? One man against forty riders? You ain't got a chance in hell."

"You pass the word, Mr. Toland. From now on I shoot on sight."

He turned around and walked off and I watched him go. Only when he was well out of sight did I lower the hammer on the rifle. Then I set about going over the camp.

The dead man had nothing on him to say who he was, but he did have five double eagles, and I took those. Then I covered his head with the blanket and went through the gear and saddlebags.

They had a good bit of food, and that was a welcome sight. I needed to be on the trail as soon as possible, but first I wanted to eat. Building up the fire, I put on coffee, fried bacon, and a big chunk of pan bread. I ate it all, then saddled both their horses.

Ketchum Mountain was a long ride and I didn't want to kill my horse getting there. Way I figured, with two extra horses I could change off when one got tired and go pretty much the whole way at a run.

With food in my belly, I retrieved my own horse and started off riding one of the others. Somewhere over by Ketchum Mountain I'd find Beth and Billy. I tried not to think about what would happen if Hank Collins found them first.

The dun under me was a good horse, and when I stuck in the spurs he tore the air. The land between the Glass Mountains and Ketchum Mountain was fine for running a horse if a man was careful, and that dun was game. After a time he lathered up, tossed his head, and I knew he was tiring. Only when he stumbled and nearly fell did I rein in and switch horses.

Ketchum Mountain was fifty miles or so north and a bit east, give or take ten miles either way. But by the time I ran both the Rocking M horses into the ground and started on my Claybank we were right there close.

Close enough to slow down and start watching for trouble. I'd never heard of Cholla Creek, but I was following along on the trail Collins left, and it was fresh. Almighty fresh.

I'd been going slow for an hour, studying the tracks, watching for trouble, when a shot rang out. It was short and sharp, the sound of a pistol, and no more than a few hundred yards away. Not knowing what to expect, I jerked my Winchester from the scabbard and stuck spurs to my claybank, charging right toward the sound of the shot. I came around a bend going full tilt. Right there, not forty yards ahead, I saw a man stretched out on the ground, another standing over him with a six-gun.

The man with the six-gun heard me coming and swung the muzzle my way. At twenty yards flame burst from the barrel and a bullet burned my shoulder. He thumbed back the hammer for a second shot.

CHAPTER 16

THE COLT EXPLODED just as the claybank's shoulder caught the man full in the chest. He went sprawling, the Colt flying from his hand. Wheeling the claybank around, I dropped to the ground.

The man was crawling for the Colt, and I yelled at him to stop. He didn't listen. His hand touched the butt, and still on his knees, he started bringing it up. I fired from the hip and he jerked under the impact of the bullet.

He was sideways to me, and my bullet caught him in the armpit, going right through his chest. An odd, questioning look came over his face. For several seconds he looked at me, then fell forward onto the ground.

The man already on the ground was Billy. Kneeling down, I rolled him over. Blood ran down the side of his face, coming from a bullet groove along his forehead. It didn't look too serious, but he was out cold. Getting my canteen, I poured water over the wound, then bandaged it as best I could.

Somewhere along that time Billy's eyes opened. It took him a minute or two to focus, and another minute to realize who I was. "Ben? God, is that you?"

"It's me. Where's Beth?"

He shook his head, grunted, and squeezed his eyes shut against the pain. "She . . . she run off into the brush there. I made a play so she could get away. She took off with Collins after her. Then the lights went out. Thought sure I was dead."

"Will you be all right for a time?"

"You know it."

Leaving Billy, I went over to where he'd pointed and started looking for sign of where Beth had run. Collins's big boot prints were the easiest to find, and I followed those, going along as fast as I dared.

There was a wetness inside my coat sleeve that I knew was blood, but it didn't feel too bad. My arm worked fine, and the pain was tolerable, so I figured the bullet couldn't have done much harm. In any case, it could wait until I found Beth.

Twenty minutes later I heard a scream, then another. I started running. There, right near a trickle of a stream, I saw Beth. She was on her back, Hank Collins atop her, tearing at her clothing. He saw me coming and rolled off Beth, jumping to his feet. He clawed for his Colt, but the loop was still over the hammer and caught as he tried to free it.

Stopping twenty feet away, I fired the Winchester from the hip. The bullet tore into his stomach and he staggered backward, but kept his feet. I fired again and he went over backward, sightless eyes staring at the sky.

Beth ran to me, shaking like a leaf. I held her for a time, feeling almighty awkward. After a bit she pulled away. "I'm sorry," she said. "It's just that I was so scared. . . ."

"He won't hurt nobody else."

Beth's voice was hard. "I'm glad. Never in my life have I wanted to see a man dead, but in this case I'm glad." Beth's face suddenly showed worry. "Is Billy all right? I heard a shot behind me when I started running."

"He's got a wicked groove along his forehead, but he'll be fine."

I turned to walk back to where Billy was and Beth gasped. "You're bleeding!"

"It's nothing."

"I'll decide that. Let me have a look."

"All right, but it can wait till we get back to Billy. You got anything in the way of food?"

"Not a thing. We've been living on what we could catch. Billy snared a jackrabbit, and caught a few fish. That's about it."

"I got enough to last us a day or two. The others'll be here by then."

"What others?"

"McKay, the Miller brothers. We'll talk about it later."

We got back to where Billy was, and I built a fire. Beth took a look at my shoulder, cleaned the bullet cut and put a bandage on it, then went to work fixing something to eat. They both ate like they hadn't seen food in a month, and I did my share as well.

With all three of us eating like that, I was thinking, McKay and the others better bring a mule train of food.

After getting her fill, Beth told me her side of what happened the night the ranch was burned. Then she asked who else got away.

I shook my head. "Chan Fowler, Tom Wooten, Travis Ward. That's all. And at least one of them was wounded. Maybe two."

"The others?"

"Dead. All except Bob Parker. He's the one sold us out. Don't know how, but he was on guard alone that night. He let the Rocking M come right up on foot."

"Well, son of a bitch," Billy said. "That ain't right, Ben. A man don't turn on his friends like that."

"One of us'll likely run into him again. Least, I sure hope so. Anyway, nothing we can do about it now. How's your leg, Billy?"

"Ah, hell, Ben. It's some sore, but I don't even miss it no more. Not much, I don't."

"How's riding a horse?"

"Took some getting used to, but things being like they are, it was learn or get killed. Nothing to it now. Walking ain't so bad, either."

"That's good," I said, " 'cause we got to move."

"Where to?"

I pointed east. "Three, maybe four miles out there."

"Hell," Billy said. "There's nothing out there but cactus and mesquite."

"Yes, sir. That's the idea. We'll find something better later. Right now I just want to get someplace where McKay can find us . . . and the Rocking M can't."

"How long before we have to leave?" Beth asked.

"The sooner the better. Why?"

"Because I'm dirty, my hair is a mess, and I smell awful. That stream over yonder widens into a little pool, and I'd like to take a bath."

I grinned. "All right. We'll fill the canteens and water the horses, then you can have a bath. Come to think of it, when you're done I reckon I'll take a turn. I ain't had a bath in two weeks."

Beth laughed. "No, really?"

"Go ahead and laugh," I said. "But I don't see nobody volunteering to sit downwind of you."

"You have a point."

I took care of filling the canteens and watering the horses, then turned the pool over to Beth. She took her time, but came back at last, looking clean and refreshed. When she was done I went down to the pool, and Billy followed soon after.

Sitting there in the cold water, I got a good look at Billy's bare leg. The stub was still an angry red along the scar, but calluses were already forming where his skin met the woolen pad he'd used to cover the inside of his pegleg.

"My foot still itches sometimes," he said, "and now and again I can feel my toes wiggle.

"Funny thing, though. It ain't near as bad as I thought it'd be. I can't run or jump worth nothing, but I can walk and ride a horse fine.

"On the other hand, if I find out for sure who the bastard was that shot me, I damn well intend to make him pay. Losing a leg mightn't be as bad as I thought, but it's bad enough."

"Ah, hell, Billy. I never worried about it. I knew you'd take it fine."

"You knew more'n I did, then. For a time there, I was wishing that bullet had gone through my head."

I grinned. "That last one near did. Best be careful what you wish for."

He rubbed at the bandage on his head. "Might be you're right. I sure got a whopper of a headache to remind me."

The day was warm, nearly hot, but the pool of water was still cold enough to make sitting there for too long uncomfortable. Neither one of us came out looking near as good as Beth, but at least our smell didn't frighten the horses.

The horse Beth and Billy had been riding was near wore out, so they each took one of the Rocking M horses and we started off straight east, riding out into cactus and brush. I wanted to get three or four miles out from nowhere and find a place to sit quiet until McKay and the others showed up.

I was in a pickle about our trail, though. On the one hand I wanted to make damn certain the Rocking M men couldn't find us, but I did want McKay to. In the end I decided to cover the trail as best I could, trusting that McKay and the Miller boys together could work things out.

Not more than a mile out we startled a deer and it bolted for cover. It didn't seem likely any Rocking M riders would be out in that godforsaken country until they came looking for Collins and the others, and I'd no idea what kind of meat Harry and Paul might bring, so when that deer bolted I snapped up my rifle and took the shot.

A tuft of hair erupted from behind the deer's shoulder. It ran another twenty yards, then folded up and skidded nose first into the ground. I gutted it right there on the spot, figuring to skin it proper once we'd made camp somewhere.

I slung the gutted deer behind my saddle, then turned the horse straight north and rode another mile. There we found enough rocky ground to cover our tracks for a time. Before leaving the rock, I cut one of the Rocking M blankets into several squares and tied a piece over each horseshoe so as to keep them from making a distinct print once we left the rocks.

It's a trick that works well in the right kind of ground. A horse, especially one with a rider, weighs more'n a little, and even with a blanket over its shoes it leaves a print in soft ground. Only, the print is spread out more, distorted, and wears away quick in the rain and wind. Unless the Rocking M had some mighty fine trackers, they wouldn't be able to follow our trail.

I only hoped McKay and the others could. Well, I could likely find them even if they couldn't find us. Leastways, that's how I was going to play it.

We went near five miles before I spotted what I hoped was a likely campsite. For most of the year, that county is dry as old bones. On account of this, most of the things growing, cholla cactus and mesquite, don't need much in the way of water. Others things, now, such as cottonwoods, need a good bit of water. So when you see a big old cottonwood growing out among the cactus and brush, you know there's some kind of water nearby.

Sometimes the water is underground and the tree has tapped it with roots. Other times there'll be a stream or a water hole feeding the cottonwood. That's what I was looking for, and that's what I found.

I saw the cottonwood from half a mile and turned my claybank's nose to point at it. Once we got closer I saw two smaller trees. Turned out there was a small water hole beneath the cottonwoods, fed by an underground spring. It wasn't much, but plenty for our needs.

Graze for the horses was a problem, but there was a bit around, enough to keep them happy for a few days. After that, I hoped to go on to a better campsite. McKay knew the country like the back of his hand, and if there was a spot around worth operating from, he'd know it or find it.

About the only drawback to the spot was lack of visibility. The land looked flat, but wasn't. It rolled and swelled gently, and the water hole was in the bottom of a long swell. At most we could see a couple of hundred yards, and the cactus and brush made even that tough.

That was a small drawback, though, especially since I could walk half a mile or so and get up high enough to see a fine stretch of country. So we settled in and made ourselves it home. First thing I did was skin out the deer and put a haunch over the fire.

Ain't many things in the world better for cooking with than mesquite wood. I've known folks who thought the taste it gave meat was too strong. Me, I couldn't get enough of it. With a big cut of that mesquite-flavored meat on my plate, a cup of strong coffee to hand, and a smoke to top it off, I was happy as a turkey in a nest of june bugs.

CHAPTER 17

FOUR DAYS PASSED before McKay and the Millers came riding into camp. And McKay wasn't happy.

"Goddang it, boss," he said, "I know you didn't want those Rocking M boys to find you, but I didn't know you were hiding from us too."

"Hiding from you? I left a trail a blind man could follow."

"Some trail. We'd still be wandering around out there if we hadn't accidentally come close enough to spot your smoke."

"I thought you could track a catfish up a muddy stream?"

"A catfish leaves a better trail. How'd you drop out of sight like that? We trailed you plain to a rocky outcropping back yonder a few miles. Then it was like you dropped off the face of the earth."

I explained the trick I'd used, and he swore. "Hell, I should've known. That ground out there's just right for a trick like that, and we were just far enough behind to let the wind play hob with things."

Harry and Paul had bought enough food to feed an army for three months. They had an extra horse to carry what they couldn't, and it was loaded down to the point of staggering. As they climbed down, Harry tossed me a fresh sack of tobacco. I caught it.

Paul dug around in the supplies and came out with a bottle of whiskey. He tossed that and I caught it as well.

"Don't reckon it's safe for none of us to get drunk out

here," he said, "but I didn't figure one bottle could hurt things."

"You figured right," I said. I popped the cork and took a long pull. It burned all the way down, hit bottom, and burned some more. "Good," I said. "Real good."

I tossed the bottle back to Paul. He took a drink and passed it around.

"How were things in Comanche Creek?" I asked.

"Hectic," Paul said. "Real hectic. When we got there the town was full of Rocking M riders. Especially the saloon. They gave us the once-over, but the brands on our horses convinced them.

"We didn't figure it'd look right to grab a bunch of supplies and hightail it right out, so we stayed the night. Me and Harry drank a couple of beers, got ourselves into a small poker game, and those Rocking M fellas got real talkative."

"That's the truth," Harry said. "They was all bragging about burning the ranch and running the Reverse Box E out of the country. Next morning, though, it was a whole 'nother story."

"What happened?"

Paul smiled wide. "Seems like somebody got in close and shot up Neal Pierce's house. Put bullets through half the windows, killed three or four prize horses, and dang near parted Pierce's hair with a bullet."

"I guess he was some put out by it, too," Harry said. "Next morning we went over to the saloon for breakfast when a fella came charging into town on a horse and told the news. In ten minutes' time there wasn't a Rocking M rider left in Comanche Creek. Reckon Pierce will keep a few more about the place from now on."

Me, I rolled a fresh cigarette, poured a healthy dollop of whiskey into my coffee. Then I leaned back and thought things out. Had to be one of our boys out there.

Likely the same man who shot up the Rocking M riders when our ranch was burned.

Had to be Fowler, Wooten, or Ward. And I was still betting on Chan Fowler. Not that Travis or Tom weren't brave enough, but it wasn't their style. No, sir, it had to be Chan Fowler.

I'd known some hardcases in my time, men who'd look right down the barrel of a gun and shoot a man who'd crossed him without a second thought. Chan Fowler was like that. He'd hired on to ride and fight for the Reverse Box E, and he'd do his part or die in the trying.

He was out there somewhere, doing his best to shake things up. Might be him and the others was riding together. In any case, he'd keep stirring up the hornets' nest until he figured the fight was over, or until he got stung to death.

And he'd figure at least some of us were still alive, so he'd be looking for us. But he'd have to keep a low profile and ride careful. All the more so since he was shooting things up in his spare time.

Chan Fowler didn't know the country. At least I didn't think so. Might be he'd traveled these parts and knew them as well as anybody, though he'd never let on that he had. Wooten wasn't much better. Travis, now, he knew the lay of the land almost as well as McKay. If they were together he could show Fowler the best places to hide . . . and to attack.

But if they weren't together, Chan Fowler was on his own. Though I doubted being alone would bother him any. Not if I read him right.

The real question was, what would he do next? He'd shot up Pierce's house, and killed a few good horses. Both acts meant to stir Pierce up rather than do any real harm.

I leaned forward so fast, coffee sloshed out of my cup. "How many of the Rocking M riders left Comanche Creek when word came about the shooting?"

Harry and Paul looked at each other. "Hell," Paul said. "Ever' last one of 'em. They all saddled up and took out like their tails was on fire."

"That's it, then," I said. "That's what Fowler had in mind."

"Fowler? You reckon it was him shot up Pierce's house?"

"You know it. And I think he had more than mischief in mind. Look at it, he don't know the country and he'd need supplies. He'd also want word on what was going on, and word of us, if it was to be had.

"He couldn't ride into Comanche Creek with twenty Rocking M riders there night and day, so he pulls this stunt. I'd bet a dollar against a stale doughnut that he was riding into Comanche Creek two hours after the Rocking M riders rode out."

"Even if that's true," Harry said, "where does it leave us? He couldn't hang around long, and by now he's dug a new hole and pulled the dirt in after him."

"Likely. I'd like to have a look-see around Comanche Creek myself though. Might be I can pick up his trail. And I'd sure like to know more about what's going on my own self."

"That don't sound too safe," McKay said. "Pierce will have more men guarding his house now, and he'll have more out scouring the hills, but there'll still be a few sitting around Comanche Creek at any given time. You go in there and get recognized it might be tough getting out again."

"Un-huh. But a good many of the Rocking M riders ain't seen me at all, and none of them've seen me with a beard. Not that it matters. I ain't going in there to be seen.

"I know a person or two who can be trusted. They can do the asking around while I sit in the shadows."

"I don't like the idea at all," Beth said. "It's too risky."

"I'll be fine. First thing, though, is to find a campsite. Something more permanent. Anybody got any ideas?"

McKay thought a minute. "How close you want to be to the Rocking M?"

"A day and a half at most. We need to be close enough to strike at a target, and far enough away to feel halfway safe."

"I know a spot about forty miles south of the Pecos, down in the Glass Mountains. It's a hell of a long way from here, but just about the right distance from the Rocking M. There's water, graze, plenty of wild game. Plenty of broken country to hide in, too."

"What if we have to retreat?"

"No problem, unless they come in with two or three hundred men. When I say that country is broken, I mean it. Most of it's dry as hell, if you don't know where to look for water. There's rattlesnakes everywhere, and not much else.

"The spot I have in mind is high up . . . kind of a big shelf overlooking a lot of country. Thing is, it looks easy to get at, but you can't reach it coming straight on. You have to go around and come up the backside, and even there, you got to know the trails. We could see riders coming for miles. Be a good spot to fight from, or we could clear out and be halfway to Mexico before anybody could stop us."

"How far from here, McKay?"

"A week, maybe. We're way the hell north of anything, and we'll have to ride wide around so nobody spots us heading that way."

"There's nothing closer?"

"Closer to here, hell yes. Closer to the Rocking M, no, sir, I'd say not."

I thought a minute. "All right, you know the country, so we'll go your way."

Then I had another thought. "Beth, there's no need for you to go along. Best thing you could do is ride over to Austin and stay there until this thing is settled."

"And what will you do in the meantime?"

"Keep fighting until Pierce gives in."

"Or until all of you are killed?"

"I ain't going about this to get myself killed. Besides, you could do us more good in Austin than hiding out in the hills. If word gets out to the right people what happened it'll stir up trouble for Pierce."

"With who?"

"The rangers, maybe even the governor. Hell, I don't know. Pierce is a big rancher, but there's limits to what he can get away with."

"Not that I've seen," Beth replied. "If the opportunity comes I'll write a letter to the governor, and even one to the rangers. My husband had friends, and maybe that will carry some weight. But I'm not going to Austin. I'm going with you and that's final."

Well, far as I could recollect, I'd never won an argument with a woman in my life. Guess there was no reason to ruin a perfect record.

"All right, so you're staying." I looked to Harry. "Dig out some of that grub and we'll eat. Come first light, we'll start south."

McKay was looking off to the south, a faraway look in his eyes. "What's bothering you?" I asked.

He shook his head. "I'm a cattleman, boss. Been one all my life. We never did get those cattle moved into that canyon. They'll be scattering now, and rustlers'll likely pick 'em to pieces. We don't settle this thing soon, we won't have a herd to worry about. The Reverse Box E will be nothing more than a bunch of empty land."

"I know," I said. "Been giving it some thought myself. If the chance comes, we'll try to round up as many head as we can and get them somewheres safe. Don't know what else to do."

"I do," McKay said. "We got to put the Rocking M in the same spot. Scatter their cattle, make them easy targets for rustlers."

"That might work," I said. "Hell, Pierce would have to

use half his men guarding the cattle. That'd sure give us a better chance."

"That's my thought. We pulled our cattle together because of the trouble. I imagine Pierce did the same. And what he didn't gather then, he'd be getting ready to now. Spring roundup ain't that far away.

"Like as not he's got three or four herds. Hell, with all his cattle he'd have to have that many. If he put 'em all together they'd graze the range bare. Yes, sir, can we scatter his cattle, it would sure give us a better chance."

"That'll be our first move," I said. "Once we get settled in a permanent camp, we'll hit his cattle."

McKay grinned. "Pierce won't like that. His cattle make him what he is. He'll take it real unkindly having them scattered all over hell and gone."

"I'll worry about that all night."

McKay laughed. "Yeah, I won't sleep a wink."

"Now that we've whupped Pierce without leaving the camp, I think it's time to eat. I'm starving to death. Thirsty, too. Hand that bottle over here."

McKay took a swig, tossed me the bottle. I took a drink, handed it on to Paul.

It all sounded easy while sitting around a fire drinking whiskey. Only, I'd been through the war and knew better. It's always easy when you're talking about it the night before.

Then morning comes and the bloody battle starts for real . . . going to see the elephant, we called it. All of a sudden the night before is a long-gone memory. When the bullets start flying there ain't one damn thing that's easy . . . except getting killed.

CHAPTER 18

WE SWUNG WELL west in our ride, skirting the border, coming down along Canyonosa Draw, then over into the Glass Mountains, and finally to the spot we were looking for. It took us near nine days of riding to get there, and we were trail-worn and tired to the bone.

But it sure enough was a fine spot. It was near three hundred feet above the trail and had an overhanging wall going up a hundred feet above that. There was a pool of water back in the rocks, shelter from the rain and sun, and anybody trying to get to us was in for a bushel of trouble.

The campsite was really little more than a wide ledge, stretching out a hundred feet or so from that overhanging wall, but it had everything a body could want. There was graze for the horses down on the western side, and even a trail a man could ride down that way if he was desperate enough.

Wild game wasn't plentiful, but there was enough about to meet our needs. Along with the supplies we'd brought, there was no worry on that score. The water hole was a big hollow in the rocks, formed by runoff from rains over God knew how many years. I worried about it going dry.

"It gets low at times," McKay said, "but I've never seen it dry. Besides, there's a small trickle of a stream not far off.

"Thing that worries me is the weather. It's already starting to warm up, and this country gets hot early and stays that way eight months out of the year. Spring'll be here soon, then summer. Believe me, boss, you don't want to spend a summer out here. Not unless you're studying up for a long stay in hell."

"Don't figure to be here that long. We're going to hit Pierce hard and often. Make him back down and shut up, or get out of the country. We can't fight a long battle. If it comes to that he'll win. No, sir, we got to hit him hard and fast and often. We got to end this thing."

"You got any ideas on how to go about it?"

"Just like you said, McKay. First we got to hit his cattle, scatter 'em over half the state. He'll have to spread himself thin to watch the cattle, and when he does, we'll hit right at him."

"You mean his ranch, where he lives? That'll be tough. No matter how many men he sends out hunting us or guarding cattle, you can bet he'll keep plenty about the place to watch over him."

I took off my hat, wiped at my forehead. My beard itched and I wanted to shave. Only, I needed the beard for my ride into Comanche Creek.

"One thing I learned in the army," I said. "There's always a way. No matter how well the enemy digs in, somewhere he's got a weak spot. All we got to do is find it, then figure out how to attack it.

"First thing is to rest and plan. We're all saddle-sore and worn out. We'll rest a day or two, plan on what to do, then we'll get about our business."

That's exactly what we did. For two days we rested, ate, and planned. McKay spent a good bit of time teaching the rest of us about the lay of the land, going over it time and again until we could all count on getting to a place and back again without help.

First thing we had to do was scout things out. We needed to know where Pierce was herding his cattle and how many men were guarding them.

"No telling how many cattle he's got, all told," I said. "Sure enough more than the Reverse Box E."

"He sent almost three thousand head up the trail last year," McKay said. "I'd say he's got near twice that many left over. He'd have to hire a bunch of extra hands to pull them all together into herds, but knowing Pierce, I'd say that wouldn't stop him."

"What's the best way to go about the scouting?"

"You still intent on riding into Comanche Creek?"

"Best way I know to be certain on some things."

"All right." McKay picked up a stick and sketched out a crude map. "You go right around this way, up along Big Canyon. That's stand-on-end country, but you can pick through it easy enough.

"Once you reach the Pecos, cross over and ride about a half mile from the north bank, heading for Comanche Creek. If Pierce has pushed any cattle north of the river, you should be able to tell.

"Harry, you and Paul point your noses right at the Reverse Box E. It's a dollar to a dime that Pierce has a sizable bunch of cattle eating Mrs. Alison's grass. It's the best graze about, and having cattle there will help him lay claim to the place should it come to that."

"What about you?" I asked.

"I'll have a look at the Rocking M, see what's going on there."

I turned to Beth. "That leaves you here with Billy."

"Like hell it does," Billy said. "I been sitting things out long enough. I'm going along on this one."

"I could use a partner," McKay said. "Only, it leaves Beth here alone. I'm not sure I like it."

"I'll be all right," Beth said. "I can use a rifle, and there's no way anyone can find me, or reach me if they do."

"You sure?" I asked.

"I am."

"Fine. But if you see anybody coming you don't know, don't be afraid to shoot. If you can't shoot, then get in the saddle and run.

"Go straight east for two days, then angle north until you

hit the Pecos. Follow that down to Langtry. Then hunt a hole and stay put. We'll find you."

"I'll be fine, Ben. Don't worry. But don't y'all be gone too long, either."

I didn't smile. "Four days, five at the most. Some of us will be back by then. Probably before."

We doled out the grub, each taking enough to last a week, leaving the bulk with Beth. Then we went about our ways, each looking for a way to hit Pierce where it hurt.

McKay had done a tolerable job giving us the lay of the land, and I picked my way through the Big Canyon country without once getting lost—though I was a mite confused for about five hours on the second day out.

At last I came up to the Pecos and crossed over. It ran west and north, and I followed it, keeping my eyes open and riding slow. Mostly I traveled at night and no more than two hours into the morning, holing up during the main part of the day.

Going straight into Comanche Creek wasn't in my plans. First I wanted a look around. I rode back into the hills where we'd driven our cattle, hoping to find a good many of them still there, but no such luck. The only Reverse Box E cattle I saw were few and far between. Like McKay feared, they were scattered to hell and gone.

I did find a trail where thirty or so head of cattle were gathered up and driven south. No telling whose cattle they were, but it smelled like the work of rustlers.

Riding along in familiar country like that, I was doing more thinking than watching, and it nearly cost me. It was the bawling of cattle that snapped me out of my daze. Bringing my eyes back into focus, I saw a rider on the skyline, driving three head over a rise.

Sticking spurs to my claybank, I darted for cover. Then I went looking for where that cowboy was driving the cattle. Skirting along his trail, but staying well back and in cover, I soon knew.

I heard the cattle before I saw them, but it still caught me off guard. Suddenly I was looking at a thousand head of Rocking M beef, spread over a good-sized area. Leaving my claybank tucked out of sight, I found a good place to stretch out on a bit of high ground.

No doubt about it. At least a thousand head, and maybe more. Neal Pierce was pulling out all the stops, bunching his cattle up right where they would do the most good. If he managed to kill all of us, he'd come out owning the Reverse Box E by right of possession.

There'd be no proof of what happened to Beth or any of us, even should rangers or other folk come asking. Pierce would be running his cattle all over Beth's land and would claim she abandoned it.

A campfire burned not far from the herd, and four cowboys sat around it. Four others were riding guard, and two more stood on high ground, each with a rifle. Neal Pierce didn't want anybody stealing his cattle.

Well, hell, I hadn't planned on stealing them. Likely they were safe from rustlers guarded like that, but it still might be I could get them running.

But not yet. First I wanted to go into Comanche Creek and have my look around. And I wanted to come into town by night, the later the better. Trouble was the last thing on my mind. All I wanted was the chance to talk to Ruby and maybe Red Heinlin.

Easing back away from the cattle, I mounted and rode off. Then I found a place well off any trail and eased down to take a nap. Going to sleep right in the middle of God only knew how many Rocking M riders sounded tough as pulling teeth. Only it wasn't. My eyes were no more than closed when sleep came.

I slept four hours, woke up stiff. Moving my head around until my neck popped helped some, but not much. An hour of being jostled about in the saddle helped, and by the time I was coming up on Comanche Creek most of the ache was gone from my joints.

Riding up behind the town, I found a place in some brush and smoked cigarettes until it was late enough. With no watch, I couldn't be certain of the time, but going by the stars it was well after midnight. Leaving the claybank where he was, I edged down into the town afoot.

Easing through an alley, I looked the town over. The only light showing came from the saloon. Getting a proper count by looking through the windows from all the way across the street was impossible, but it didn't seem too many people were inside.

No matter. Going in through the front door wasn't in my plans. If there was one building I knew well in Comanche Creek, it was the saloon.

I worked my way down the street away from the saloon, and darted across. A dog barked loudly, but that was the only sound. A full moon was trying to come from behind some clouds, and I crossed my fingers, hoping it would stay put for an hour or two. I went around to the back of the saloon, eased up the back stairs and slowly opened the door at the top of the landing.

Opening the door no more'n a crack, I peeked through. The hallway was empty, lit dimly by two wall-mounted lamps. The thong was already off my Colt, and I eased the heavy pistol from the holster, holding it down by my side. Fast wasn't one of my strong suits, and if I needed that six-gun I didn't want to go fumbling with a holster.

I went quietly down the hall and tapped lightly on Ruby's door. Her voice rang out, asking who it was. Not wanting to yell out my name, I kept silent, tapped a little louder. I heard movement from inside, then the door suddenly opened a foot or so, framing Ruby's face.

She started to snap out something nasty, then her eyes went wide as she recognized me. "Ben? Oh, God, what are you doing here?"

"I need to talk to you."

Her voice was a whisper. "I got company in here. He's dead drunk and asleep . . . or passed out, but he rides for Neal Pierce."

"Damn it! I never thought of that."

"What, did you think I'd be sitting around pining for you? Bringing men up here is my business. Go on out there on the landing and I'll try to get rid of him."

Easing back down the hallway, I went out the door, leaving it open a crack to watch what happened. Five minutes later a half-drunk cowboy came stumbling out, Ruby helping him along.

"Dang it, Ruby," he said. "I don't see why you're a-kicking me out. I got money."

"And I got the belly gripes something awful. That's no fun for either of us. You come on back another night."

He rubbed a big hand over his face, reached out to steady himself against the wall. "Guess I could use me another shot of rotgut or two."

"Sure you could. Go on downstairs and make use of your money. I ain't fit company feeling like I am."

He walked away, staggering once, went down the stairs. It took me about three seconds to run down the hallway and get inside Ruby's room.

She looked at me hard, hands on her hips. "It's not that I ain't glad to see you," she said, "but what the hell kind of a fool thing are you doing?"

"Huh, what do you mean?"

"I mean coming into Comanche Creek like this. The Rocking M is up in arms, and all they talk about is finding you and that Alison woman."

"You mightn't believe it, Ruby, but it ain't been me stirring up no trouble. Leastways, not yet it ain't."

"I know that," she said, "but they don't."

"You know it? How's that?"

"Couple of fellas came riding into town a spell back

while the Rocking M riders were off in a tizzy to find out
who shot up Pierce's house. They bought up half the supplies the mercantile had, then came to see me. One was
named Fowler and the other Wooten. Fowler was just about
the scariest man I ever met."

"How'd they know to come see you?"

"I asked them the same thing. They said one of the men
they worked with spoke of you seeing a red-light woman
named Ruby. So they took a chance that I wouldn't go running to the Rocking M."

"What did they have to say?"

"Just that they'd be around. Said something about having a camp where you were going to take the cattle. They
wouldn't tell me more than that."

"Playing it safe. They wanted to get word to me, but they
didn't know if you could be trusted."

"Do you know where they meant?"

"I know."

"Don't suppose you're going to tell me, either."

I laughed. "Ruby, I like you. I really do. And I got no
doubts that you like me. But you like money too."

She pouted, looked up at me. "You think I'd sell you out
to the Rocking M?"

"Would you?"

"No. Well, I don't think I would."

I smiled.

She laughed. "I don't suppose you have time for a little
fun before you leave?"

I sighed. "You don't know how tempting that is, but I
reckon not. Can you tell me what Pierce has been up to
the last couple of weeks?"

"Not much. He's hired more men. Quite a few more.
They found some of their men shot up a few days back.
Hank Collins and a couple of others were killed. Another
came straggling in with his feet bleeding so bad he couldn't
stand up.

"Brice Campbell seems to be the calmest of the lot. He says he almost killed you once, and next time he won't miss."

That puzzled me for a second. Then I remembered the ride up to San Angelo. It must have been Campbell that shot my horse from under me. Well, he was truthful enough about the first part, he had come close to killing me. It was up to me to make damn sure he didn't get another chance.

"Thanks, Ruby. You been a help."

"Do you have to leave so soon?"

"Un-huh. I need to make another stop before daylight, and time's a-wasting."

She stood up on tiptoe and gave me a quick kiss. "Get rid of that brush pile before you come back. You look like an old bear."

"I am an old bear."

"Maybe. But you still have the sharpest claws in the woods."

"Thanks, Ruby. That's good to hear, even if it ain't true."

Slipping out the way I came in, I worked around to Red Heinlin's house. It took a few minutes of tapping on his window, but at last a light came on. A minute later Red opened the door, a big shotgun in his hands.

When he realized who I was, he looked both ways and quickly let me inside. We talked for a time, and I asked if he had anybody staying out in the place he let me use while working for him.

"Nope. Haven't found anybody else who wanted to work bad enough to hire on. Risky you staying there, isn't it?"

"There's no need for you to get involved at all, Red. Say the word and I'll ride away and not come back."

"What do you need?"

"My horse is hid away safe, but I'm not. If you can let me stay out there until tomorrow night and make a stop at the mercantile sometime through the day, I'd sure be obliged."

"I heard talk about them burning out Beth Alison. Just tell me what you need, Ben."

"Dynamite. Couple of dozen sticks, along with caps and plenty of fuse."

"Dynamite? What in the world have you got planned?"

"Just going to scare some cattle, is all."

"Rocking M cattle?"

"Un-huh. I figure turnabout is fair play."

Red smiled. "You go on out and get settled in. I'll bring you some breakfast when it's time."

"Best make it lunch. I haven't slept much the last couple of days."

"All right, lunch it is."

"Thanks, Red. Ain't many who'd do half as much."

"Protecting my own interests, is all. You're the only man in town who'll work at the wages I pay. Now get on out there and go to sleep."

I got on out there and stretched out on the best bed I'd seen in weeks. Sleep came fast and sound. Neal Pierce and his whole bunch could've stormed in and I wouldn't have stirred a bit.

CHAPTER 19

I'D LIKELY HAVE slept the day away had Red not half beat the door down getting me awake. Staggering to the door with Colt in hand, I opened it slowly. Red was there, along with his missus. She held a big plate of food in each hand, and Red had a wooden box tucked under one arm.

"I was beginning to think you'd died in there," he said. "Never saw a man sleep so sound."

"Ain't my way most times," I said. "Guess all that sleeping in snatches on hard ground finally caught me."

Mrs. Heinlin smiled as I let them both in. "I hope you're hungry, Mr. Hawkins."

"Yes, ma'am. And if that tastes even half as good as it smells, I'll likely ask for seconds."

"You go right ahead. There's plenty."

She set the food down on the table, and I sat down behind it. "Ma'am, I'm sure sorry about barging in on you all like this. I just didn't know where else to turn."

"Red likes you," she said. "That's good enough for me." She pointed at the box Red had set on the end of the table. "I'm not sure I like having that around, though. It makes me nervous."

"The dynamite?"

Red nodded. "They had eighteen sticks in the box, so I went ahead and bought them all. Got a hundred feet of fuse, and two dozen blasting caps in the house. I'll bring 'em out later."

"Thanks, Red. I appreciate it. You sure it won't come back on you when I go to using this stuff?"

"Shouldn't. You wouldn't believe how much dynamite the mercantile sells. You know how to use it?"

"Sure. Nothing to it, really. Crimp a fuse into a cap, slip the cap into the stick of dynamite, strike a lucifer, and let it fly. Long as it's fresh, there's nothing to worry about. The blasting caps are trickier than the dynamite."

"I've heard it goes bad if it gets too old," Red said. "Don't know as I'd want to fool with it."

I talked while I ate. "You heard right. It gets too old or too hot and it can start to sweat. And what it sweats is nitroglycerin. When it gets like that, it can blow if you sneeze at it."

"New or old," he said, "you can have it."

Mrs. Heinlin went out, came back a couple of minutes later with a pot of coffee and a cup.

"Thank you, ma'am," I said. "That'll finish things off just right."

I had both plates near clean, and Mrs. Heinlin took them out and refilled them without my asking. By the time those two were clean I was full to bursting. Me and Red talked for a time, then he went back down to the smithy, wanting to get caught up.

The rest of the day went by slow, but I waited until well after dark before leaving. I should've waited longer. Now, Comanche Creek was a small town, but with all the riders working for the Rocking M, it was never empty. I was going down a side street, looking for a likely spot to cross over and get back to my horse, when I saw a man coming toward me.

It was dark, but the moon was bright, and this time there were no clouds to hide it. Shifting the dynamite under my left arm, and holding the small package of fuse and caps in my left hand, I kept walking. After pulling my hat low, I eased the thong off my Colt, let my hand rest on the butt.

We drew closer; he glanced at me, mumbled a greeting,

then looked again, sharper. My beard didn't help worth a damn. "Wait a minute, ain't you that Ben Hawk . . . ?"

He grabbed for his Colt as he spoke, but mine was already at hand. Not wanting to risk a shot, I pulled it free and swung hard, catching the man on the side of the jaw. He went down without a sound.

His Colt wasn't so cooperative. It came free of the holster and struck the boardwalk. He'd either cocked it, or was fool enough to have a round under the hammer. All I knew for certain was that it exploded when it hit, the bullet thunking into the wall near my head.

Before the shot, the town had been noisy. There'd been laughter and music coming from the saloon, and a general hubbub of conversation coming from the few men walking about outside. When that Colt exploded, the whole town went quiet.

It didn't last long. Men poured from the saloon, looking this way and that, most with guns in hand. I swore.

It wouldn't have mattered so much except that I was on the wrong side of the main drag. To get to my claybank, I had to cross over, and I had to do it before the Rocking M men spread out to cover the town.

I was a good bit down from the saloon. Far enough to make a pistol shot from there difficult. "Ah, hell," I said aloud. Then I took a breath and darted across the street . . . not an easy thing to do carrying the dynamite.

Yet I was better than halfway across before anyone spotted me. Then someone yelled, "There he is."

A Colt boomed, and a bullet kicked up dirt right in front of me. Two more shots sounded, one bullet whizzing by my face, the second tugging at my hat. Then I was in the alley and running flat out.

My claybank was where I'd left it, and I wasted no time getting in the saddle and sticking in the spurs. That claybank had to be tired, hungry, and thirsty from being left tied and saddled all day, but he took off like he knew trouble was coming.

Two hours later we stopped for a time, and I let the claybank graze and drink. Then it was back in the saddle. Along about midnight I was a mile away from the Rocking M herd, doing my best to rig several sticks of dynamite by the light of the moon.

When they were ready, I climbed back in the saddle, rode to within two hundred yards of the herd. Leaving the claybank, I went ahead on foot until I found a spot where I could look things over.

A couple of things had changed. It was hard to tell in the moonlight, but the herd looked bigger, like maybe two or three hundred head had been driven in during the day.

The campfire was going strong, and sitting right nearby was a chuckwagon. Now, a lot of small ranchers used anything they had to carry grub about, sometimes mounting an old cabinet on the back to give them some drawer space.

The Rocking M had the real thing. It looked to be built of Osage orangewood, had metal axles, and an extra team of horses to pull the added weight. There was a bed wagon not far back, and maybe fourteen cowboys, counting those riding herd and standing guard.

Looked to me like they were planning a drive. It was early to be thinking such a thing, though the truth was I'd long since lost track of the date. But it made sense. The best way for Pierce to keep his cattle safe was to sell off any surplus.

And hell, it was a long, long drive up the trail to market. He could have the men take their time, let the cattle fatten along the way, and still be the first herd to come in. In the process he'd make a bankful of money.

The rule of thumb is six cowhands to every thousand head of cattle on a drive. Throw in a ramrod, a cook, a wrangler, a cook's helper to drive the hooligan wagon, and that makes ten men. With this herd they'd want a couple more—or several more—since they might be attacked.

When a horse whinnied and I saw the remuda out yonder, I knew they were planning a drive. Way it looked, they were ready to go. Well, I'd have to see what I could do about that.

I waited until the fire burned down and everybody was a-bed except those riding night guard. I had five sticks of dynamite fused and capped. Two of them I tied together, leaving that fuse long. I wanted it to burn at least three or four minutes. The fuses on the last three sticks I cut down short, wanting them to blow as soon as they hit.

Coming up on the backside of the chuckwagon was easy enough. There I lit the fuse on the two sticks of dynamite I'd lashed together and tossed them inside. After that I hustled away, circling around to a spot close to the herd. A horse came out of the darkness, its rider singing softly to keep the cattle calm.

I fell flat, holding my breath until the rider was well away. Then I got a match ready and waited. It seemed to take forever, but just when I was beginning to think something had gone wrong, the chuckwagon erupted in a ball of flame and flying wood.

The sound of the explosion hit my ears and I winced. Lighting the fuses on the remaining sticks of dynamite, I threw them into the herd, one left, one right, and the last straight ahead, putting everything I had into the throw.

Then I was running. Behind me the sticks of dynamite exploded one after another. The sound was deafening, but not much louder than the sudden bawling and mad stampeding of well over a thousand cattle.

The three separate explosions sent the cattle in a dozen directions, and too damn many of them came my way. The full moon was low in the sky, but still bright enough to make me a fine target. Right then I didn't care. The cattle were a bigger danger than a bullet . . . leastways, that's what I thought at the time.

Plainly put, running ain't a thing I've ever been real good at. I hadn't gone fifty yards before I was flat winded, sucking air like a horse with the ague. Only the ground was rumbling, cowboys were yelling their heads off and firing guns, and the cattle were gaining on me. So I kept running.

A thousand-pound steer rushed by so close it staggered me, and then I reached cover. As I jumped into the rocks a bullet came from out of nowhere and burned a bloody path along my left calf. I stumbled, fell, banged my shoulder hard.

For two minutes I stayed down, wanting to swear, unable to find enough air to get the words out. My lungs burned more'n the wound to my leg, and sitting a spell seemed safe enough. Those cowboys had a lot more to worry about than who set off the dynamite, and until things settled down a good bit, they wouldn't even start searching for me.

Not wanting to press my luck, I tied my bandanna tight around my calf, then hobbled off as soon as my lungs started working right. Once back in the saddle I rode south, crossed the Pecos about dawn, and pushed on another two hours.

I made camp in a spot as out of the way as I could find and built a small fire. Building a fire was taking a chance, but the wound on my leg needed cleaning, and I needed coffee.

The bullet had cut a little deeper than I'd thought, creasing the muscle before going about its way, but it wasn't too serious. Mostly it meant my left leg was going to be stiff for a couple of weeks.

Serious or not, it hurt like hell, and I did a lot of teeth gritting and swearing before I had it cleaned and bandaged proper.

While the fire was going, I made coffee and fried a pan

full of bacon. Biscuits would've gone fine with the bacon, but they were too much trouble and I was tired. I ate the bacon, drank half a pot of coffee, smoked two cigarettes, then crawled inside my blankets and went to sleep.

My leg throbbed, my shoulder hurt, and my eyes felt like they were full of sand. But after a time tiredness won out over pain and I drifted off to a fitful sleep.

CHAPTER 20

MY EYES OPENED suddenly. Somehow I knew it was a sound that awakened me, though I couldn't say what kind of sound it might have been. Then it came again. It was the sound of something big moving slowly through the brush.

Now, pillows are hard to come by out there on the range, so I'd made do with resting my head on my saddle. And before going to sleep I'd hung my Colt from the saddle horn, letting it drape down where it would be close at hand. Now I slid my hand up slowly, eased the Colt out of the holster and under the blanket.

Through half-closed eyes, I saw a shape moving in the brush. The shape of a man. He hadn't seen the camp yet, but in another step or two he would be in the open and looking right at me.

He took the step and I rolled, Colt coming into line and hammer going back to full cock. His rifle came up at the same time, the muzzle swinging to cover me. My finger was squeezing the trigger, but somehow, some way, I stopped the squeeze just before the Colt exploded.

There, right in the sights of my Colt, stood Johnny Stevens. He jerked a little, like maybe he'd had the same trouble not firing at me. For a time we looked at each other, weapons still pointed.

"Ben," he said, "is that you?"

"It's me, Johnny."

"What do we do now?"

That took some thinking. "Any reason why we can't have a truce?"

"None that I can think of, I guess. Long enough to have a bit of coffee, anyway."

I eased down the hammer, lowered the Colt. Johnny did the same with the rifle. He came over and sat across the fire from me. We were both quiet while I added sticks and brought the fire to life. That done, I took a long drink from my canteen, rolled a cigarette.

"How'd you find me?" I asked.

Johnny shrugged. "Saw smoke earlier, or thought I did. Had to come back this way and figured I'd check it out."

"I'm glad you didn't have a pack of riders along."

"Usually do. This time I didn't, is all. That you been stirring up all the trouble?"

"Not all of it."

"I don't see how you can side with fencing in the range, Ben. Hell, that'll be the end of everything. When the free range goes what'll they need cowboys for?

"It ain't right, Ben. This range has always been free and open. It ain't right."

"You burning us out and trying to kill Beth Alison is right?"

Johnny reddened. "I ain't had no part in trying to kill a woman, and I never would."

"Were you there when they burned us out?"

"I was. Can't say I'm proud of the way we went about it, but we didn't kill nobody without a gun in his hand."

"All right."

When the coffee was ready I filled Johnny's cup, then my own. He sipped, rolled a cigarette, struck a match.

"Ben, don't it mean nothin' to you? Putting up that damned barbed wire, I mean. You can't like the stuff?"

I sighed and sipped. "It ain't a matter of liking, Johnny, it's a matter of accepting. Barbed wire's coming, whether I like it or not. If we don't put it up, somebody else will. We ain't far from having all the free range everywhere fenced in. You can't stop a thing like that once it gets a toehold."

"How's a man to get his cattle to market?"

"By railroad. That's coming, too."

"I don't care, Ben. Cutting up this country with wire will spoil it. Won't be nothing left but farmers and small ranchers. Hell, a man'll have to go ten miles out of his way just to go see a neighbor.

"And railroads be damned, it's driving the herds to market that makes money. Right now beef cattle are worth four times as much at end of trail as they are here."

I flipped my cigarette into the fire. "You ever been up the Chisholm Trail, Johnny?"

He poked at the fire with a stick. "No, sir, I ain't. But I been on shorter drives."

"I been up the trail, Johnny. More times than I care to count. The Chisholm Trail ain't nothing more than two dozen ways for a cowboy to get hurt or killed. It's stampedes, rustlers, swollen rivers, snakes, lightning storms, and twisters. I've seen men killed by each and every one, and a few other ways besides.

"I ain't never had an easy trip up the trail, Johnny. If it ain't hot as hell and so dusty a man can't draw air, it's cold and wet and plain damn miserable. It's sleeping on hard ground and eating harder biscuits. All so a bunch of cattle can make another man rich.

"I ain't saying I like barbed wire, Johnny, but if I never have to drive a bunch of mule-ornery cattle north again, it'll be too soon.

"You ever hear cowboys sit and argue which is dumber, a horse or a cow? I'll tell you, Johnny, the dumbest thing going up that trail to market ain't a horse nor a cow. It's the damn fool of a cowboy willing to risk his life for thirty dollars a month and food.

"No, sir, I ain't saying I like anything about barbed wire.

But I ain't much on riding drag all the way to Kansas, neither."

Johnny looked at me over his coffee cup. "Tell yourself that if you want, Ben. Me, I think you got cattle in the blood. You're fightin' for the Reverse Box E on account of Billy. And on account of pure damned cussedness."

I had to smile. "I'd not admit it, even to you. But one thing I know, Johnny. Barbed wire's coming, no matter what any of us think about it.

"Besides, this ain't about wire no more. Pierce came at us, and now we got to come back at him. When it's over there won't be but one big ranch hereabouts."

"It'll be the Rocking M, Ben. We got too many men and too much money."

"If that's how the chips fall, then so be it. But don't bet your wages on it, Johnny. We're a long way from giving up."

Johnny finished his coffee and stood up. "Ben, I got to say this. I know we been *compañeros,* but friends or not, you and me can't have no more truces. Mr. Pierce mightn't be right in everything, but he pays my wages."

"I know, Johnny. Far as I'm concerned, we're still friends. You, me, and Billy."

"Even if one of us has to kill the other?"

"Hell, yes, Johnny. Why not?"

He grinned a little, nodded, started to turn away, then looked back at me. "You don't mind my saying so, you look like hell, Ben."

"I feel like hell, Johnny."

"Two or three hours from now I'll have to say I saw you."

"I'll be long gone."

He nodded. "Be seeing you, Ben."

"See you, Johnny."

He walked out to wherever his horse was, and for a time I sat there, wondering how in hell it all came to this. No matter. We'd each chosen our side . . . though sometimes I doubted we had any choice at all.

We each went our way through circumstance and, once there, made a stand and stayed our course.

Johnny didn't want to kill me or Billy, and we felt the same way. Hell, I didn't even want to be working for the Reverse Box E. I'd a thousand times rather have been pounding iron in a smithy, or maybe riding an acre or two of my own range, catching a few wild horses now and again, selling them off for pocket money.

I packed up and rode out of there, taking pains to cover my trail. Johnny would give me the two or three hours he promised, then he'd tell Brice Campbell or Neal Pierce about running into me. By the time they came looking, I wanted to be long gone.

I spent most of the day riding here and yon, leaving a trail that'd take even a good tracker days to work out, or so I thought, then I started looking for that box canyon. I'd told Ruby I knew where it was, but that hadn't been quite true.

McKay had told me more or less how to find it, but telling and doing are two different things. It was near noon the next day before I found it, and even then I rode by the opening twice before realizing what it was.

Thing is, the only tracks going in or coming out of the box canyon belonged to unshod horses and cattle. Try as I might, I couldn't pick out a single track of a shod horse. And truth be told, I hadn't really expected to . . . unless they belonged to a Rocking M rider going in to see who was home.

No, sir, Chan Fowler wasn't the kind of man to pin himself inside a box canyon. He'd told Ruby enough to make me look there, but not because he was waiting inside. He'd be about somewhere, close enough to watch the entrance if I was any judge. But he'd not be inside.

I was sitting my horse, thinking hard, wondering where

Fowler would be, when I heard a shout. Looking that way, I saw a man standing out in the open some two hundred yards away. He waved his rifle over his head a couple of times, then eased back into cover.

He was too far away to recognize. Easing my rifle from the scabbard, I walked my claybank toward him.

Now, most times I'd figure walking right at somebody like that would be foolish. Only from where he was, I'd been an almighty easy target for a fair shot with a rifle. So I rode that way slow, hoping it was Chan Fowler doing the yelling.

Turned out it was Tom Wooten. He hadn't been certain who I was, so Chan Fowler had laid up in the rocks with his Winchester, just in case I turned out to be unfriendly. Once they realized who I was, Chan came down.

"Whoee," Tom said. "It sure is good to see you, boss. I was beginning to think me and Chan were the only two Reverse Box E riders left."

"We set up a camp back yonder in the rocks," Chan said. "There's coffee on and you look like you could use a cup."

"I could, at that. Lead the way."

He did. Digging my cup out, I poured it full of coffee and sat down. I rolled a cigarette and looked around. It was a fine camp, set up high where they could watch the country, but with a quick way out the back side. There weren't as many supplies in camp as I'd expected, and I asked about it.

"Too hard to lay low with a pack mule in tow," Chan said. "We got a cache about ten miles east, and another south a piece. If we got to cut and run in a hurry, we'll still have those to fall back on."

It made good sense, and I wished we'd thought to do the same. I told them about Beth and the others.

"Billy's up and about?" Tom asked. "I'd never have believed it. I only talked to him once, but he sure seemed in poor shape."

"Getting out of that house and onto a horse was probably the best thing could happen to him," I said. "Hell, being cooped up like that would kill a body all by itself."

"I've never been laid up," Chan said. "Spent six months in jail one time. That's as close to dying as I ever want to come."

"Either of you seen Travis?" I asked. "McKay figured he got away."

Tom's face went glum. "You go back over yonder about fifty yards, you'll find his grave. He was hit hard, but he lived long enough to show us this place."

"He was a game kid," Chan said. "Game right up to the end."

"He'd do to ride the river with," I said.

Chan's face was hard. "I'll kill any man says different."

I stayed the night with Tom and Chan. Come morning we packed up and started south. We'd been in the saddle for no more than a minute before Chan suddenly stopped and looked northeast.

"Thought I saw something moving," he said. "About a mile yonder."

We watched the area for five minutes, saw nothing. "Must have been a cow," he said. "Guess I'm getting jumpy."

"Being jumpy is the best way I know to stay alive," I said. "This is a big, wide, wild country, but that don't mean we can't be found."

We took to riding again. Along about midmorning we cut the trail of fifty or more driven cattle, and maybe a dozen horses. The trail was headed west and a little south, right toward the border.

"Rustlers," I said. "Got to be."

Chan nodded. "There's plenty about. Most of 'em stealing Reverse Box E cattle."

"How old you figure that trail is?"

"Three hours. Any fresher and we'd be knee deep in cattle."

"You two in the mood to shake up a few rustlers?"

"Been wanting to do just that," Tom said. "Never could abide a cow thief."

We followed the trail, pushing as hard as we dared. Chan kept glancing toward the northeast, unable to shake the feeling we were being followed.

Just over two hours later we were stretched out on the rimrock, looking down on the cattle we were trailing. They were most of five hundred yards away, still being pushed hard. I counted fourteen men pushing them.

"We could circle around and get on that high ground there in front of the herd," Chan said. "Should be able to empty four or five saddles before they know what's happening."

It wasn't such a bad idea, at that. If nothing else, it would let the rustlers know the Reverse Box E cattle didn't come without a price tag. Then one of the rustlers turned in the saddle and looked more or less our way. It was hard to tell from the distance, but I'd swear it was Rio Grande Jim Macklin.

Tom came up to one knee, starting to move back toward the horses. He'd no more than got up when his chest seemed to erupt and he flew backward, dead before he hit. It seemed a long time before the sound of the rifle shot reached our ears.

We scooted behind a lip in the rimrock, but there was nowhere to go beyond it. The closest cover was fifty yards back, and even crawling we'd be easy targets.

"*Son of a bitch!*" I yelled. "Where's that coming from?"

"Way the hell over yonder," Chan said. "There on that far rim."

A bullet tore into the rock, inches from my face. If it hadn't been for that small lip rising up, we'd both have joined Tom in short order.

I'd no more than thought of Tom when another bullet tore through his body. We were close enough to know he was dead, but whoever was doing the shooting wanted to make sure.

"Must be a Sharps," I said. "You think it's one of the rustlers?"

"It's a Creedmore," Chan said. "Used to have one, so I know the sound. It fires a .45/70 round, and a good shot can cut the wing off a fly at half a mile."

"And that's no rustler. It's whoever's been trailing us all morning. It's my fault, too. I knew damn well somebody was out there."

"It's nobody's fault," I said. "But we got to get off this rimrock or die. Sooner or later he'll drop a bullet on one of us."

He would, too. That lip of rock in front of us was no more than a foot high, and the bushwhacker was six, maybe seven hundred yards off. At that range any bullet would be dropping fast, and once he got the range, that lip of rock wouldn't protect us at all.

We both had our rifles, but a Winchester wasn't worth a damn at that range. Still, might be we could stir him up some. "I hear you're a fine shot yourself," I said. "Think you can put a bullet close to that fellow?"

Chan shook his head. "With this popgun? I can let him know he's being shot at, but I sure as hell won't hit him."

"Just come close. Soon as you pull the trigger I'm going to break for the rocks over to my left. If I can get there, I'll cut down through that cover and run. Hell, maybe he'll stay there long enough for me to get in range. Can you hold out for ten minutes or so?"

"That depends on how good he is. Once you're gone, I can scoot up right behind the rock here and that'll make it tougher on him. But don't go lollygagging around."

"You know it," I said. "Just make him miss his first shot. With a little luck I can be under cover before he reloads."

"All right. You ready?"

"Ready as I'll ever be."

"It'll take my bullet a while to get there," Chan said. "Take two breaths before you start running."

I nodded. Chan raised the sights on his Winchester, eased the barrel over the lip of rock. He drew in a deep breath, let half of it out. A bullet spanged off the rock right in front of us. Chan flinched, steadied his sights again, and squeezed the trigger. I took a deep breath, let it out, drew in a second, then jumped to my feet and hit running.

CHAPTER 21

THE ONE THING I'd forgotten about was my leg. It had already begun to scab over and stiffen up, and the first hard, running step I took tore it wide open. The pain was sharp enough to make me stagger. Chan's bullet must have come close enough to startle whoever was over there, though, because he didn't nail me during that stagger.

I caught my balance and ran, ignoring the pain in my leg. Five strides later a bullet hit the rock five feet in front of me, ricocheted off with a nasty whine. Behind me, I heard Chan fire twice more.

Those rocks seemed forever away. I ran for all I was worth, but it was like being stuck in the mud. Another bullet hit right between my feet, stinging my legs with flying rock. Then I was in the boulders and relatively safe. I didn't slow down.

From there I had brush and cover near all the way to where the gunman was hiding. How far did I have to run? Eight, maybe nine hundred yards. That, anyway. He'd have a quick way out, but if I could reach that yonder ridge before he took it, I'd have a shot. Maybe not much of a shot, but still a shot.

I hate running. Even as a kid I was no good at it. Now I was older than half the trees in Texas, and my body just wasn't up to the task. But I ignored my body and ran anyway.

Blood ran down my leg and squished in my boot with every step. My lungs hurt, my throat burned. Then my toe caught on something and I fell headfirst, hitting hard, skinning my left hand and dropping my rifle.

I was up and running again without thought. I brushed a cholla cactus and the thorns dug into my left arm. Some folks call cholla the "jumping cactus," others call it "porcupine cactus," both for the same reason. The dense thorns are like quills on a porcupine. They have barbed ends that stick right into the skin and stay there. And they hurt like blue hell.

Then I was on the ridge, my chest heaving and red spots flashing in front of my eyes. Something trickled down from my nose and touched my lips. Salty. It tasted salty. Then I saw the man. He was running full tilt, right toward his horse.

My rifle came up by itself. Only, I couldn't hold a breath, and my hands were shaking. I jerked the trigger and the bullet missed him by ten feet. His head turned to look my way and I saw it was Brice Campbell.

He was a bit under two hundred yards away, and most times I couldn't miss a shot like that. But it took all I had to jack another round into the chamber.

Dropping down on my ass, and steadying the rifle by putting my elbows on my knees, I forced myself to hold a quick breath and squeezed the trigger just as Campbell's foot went into the stirrup. The bullet slammed him against his horse and he fell.

Before I could get a third shot off he was up and in the saddle, hightailing it away. I snapped off two more shots, missing wildly.

My head was spinning like a top. I tried to stand up, lost my footing, and fell. "The . . . hell . . . with it," I gasped. Facedown in the dirt, I waited for my chest to stop heaving and my body to stop hurting. Neither one happened anytime soon.

Next thing I knew, Chan Fowler was there, helping me up. My eyes still wouldn't focus. He was looking me up and down, saying something I couldn't make out. He said it several times before the words made sense.

"Are you hit?" he was saying. "Where are you hit?"

"Huh, I ain't hit. I don't think so, anyway."

"Hell, man, you're covered with blood."

Looking down, I saw my shirtfront was soaked with blood. Then I dabbed at my nose with the back of my hand. It came away red. "Nosebleed," I said. "Guess something popped in there."

Chan had brought the horses, and he poured water from a canteen on his bandanna, gave it to me. "Pinch your nose shut with it," he said. "It'll stop in a minute."

It did. My legs were still shaky and I had to sit down. "Next time," I said, "you do the running and I'll cover you."

"Deal. Did you see who it was?"

"Brice Campbell. Saw him plain."

"Damn. We got to move, Hawkins. He'll be back with help."

My arm burned like fire where the cholla needles were embedded. "Not anytime soon, he won't. Not with a bullet in his hide."

"You hit him!"

"Don't know how bad, but I hit him."

"There's a trickle of water a mile or so back," Chan said. "We best get over there and get you fixed up."

I nodded. "What about the rustlers? Any of them cut free of the cattle?"

"Nope. When they realized they weren't being shot at, they started the cattle running and made tracks."

We rode over to the water Chan remembered. Chan built a fire while I stripped down. After he worked the thorns from my arm and rebandaged my leg, I washed off and changed my shirt. Chan built a small fire and put coffee on, then got back in the saddle.

"Where you headed?" I asked.

"You rest up. I'm going to see that Tom's covered proper.

I rested, drank a cup of coffee when it was ready. Chan came back an hour later, poured a cup of his own. We drank the coffeepot dry, smoked, talked. "I don't know which I want most right now," I said, "a shot of whiskey, or a chance to get back at the Rocking M."

Chan looked into the fire for a full minute, then raised his eyes to meet mine. "I know a spot where we might get both," he said. "That interest you?"

"You know it does. Trot it out and run it around the corral once or twice and we'll see how it prances."

Chan took out a cigar, lit it. "Me and Tom did a good bit of running about, getting to know the country, looking for ways to hit back at the Rocking M. And looking for you all, for that matter.

"A week or so back we trailed some riders, wanting to know who they were and where they were headed. We stumbled onto a little place about two days' ride from here, over near the Mexican border.

"Ain't much. Just a small saloon built of adobe, and maybe half a dozen houses built the same way, all scattered along a small creek. Don't even know if it's got a name. Sure as hell ain't got a store nor anyplace to buy supplies."

"What makes you think we'll find Rocking M riders there?"

Chan shrugged. "We went over by there twice, and each time there was four or five Rocking M horses tied in front of the saloon. Tell you the truth, my guess would be it's a hangout for rustlers. It's right near the border, and sure as anything it ain't a place folks go to sightsee. Besides, me and Tom got to following every trail we cut that looked like rustlers', and a good many went right through that little burg."

"Might be Pierce has hired a few men who're working both sides of the street."

I sipped my coffee, straightened my left leg, rubbed at my arm. I hurt all over, and it was making me mad. "It'll put us a few days late getting back to the others," I said, "but what the hell. Let's go take a look."

We saddled up and rode out, Chan leading the way.

We came into the small town, if you wanted to call it that, along about noon, two full days after the shoot-out with Brice Campbell.

We didn't go in, but looked things over from three hundred yards away. It was just as Chan had described it: a dirt-poor little village with nothing going for it except a saloon and a quick trip across the border.

Eight horses were tied up in front of the saloon, but from where we sat, neither of us could read the brands. A man came out of the saloon, stepped around the corner of the building, unbuttoned his pants, and wet down the dirt.

"How do you want to go about it?" Chan asked.

"You as good with that Colt as you are with a rifle?"

"Better, I'd say."

I slipped my Winchester from the scabbard, jacked a round into the chamber. "Then let's go to the front door and see if they invite us in. Unless you got a better idea?"

"Nope. Let's do 'er."

We rode down to the saloon side by side. An old Mexican man came out of an adobe hut, took one look at us, and went back inside. A flock of chickens came scattering from some brush, followed by a mangy-looking hound, his mouth full of tail feathers.

Once close enough, we read the brands of the horses tied in front of the saloon. Five of them belonged to Rocking M riders. "Looks like the odds are wrong," Chan said. "Might be we ought to wait a spell."

"Might be more Rocking M riders come along if we do that."

"Yes, sir, that's what I mean. They need four or five more men on their side to even things up."

I had to smile. "No use being hogs about it," I said.

"McKay and the others would be put out if we took their share."

"Reckon we'll have to make do with just the five, then."

"I reckon."

We tied our horses in front of the saloon and Chan slipped the thong off his Colt. The door to the saloon was off the hinges and propped against the wall. An old blanket hung over the opening in its place. I pushed it aside and stepped through.

It was close inside. The whole building was less than forty feet long and twenty-five feet deep. The bar was nothing more than a dozen barrels lined up side by side with planks across the top. Half a dozen beat-up, stained tables filled the room. Three men stood at the bar, four others sat playing cards fifteen feet to my right, and another man sat alone in a far corner.

Three Mexicans were at another table, and a balding man with a big belly stood behind the bar, wiping a dirty glass with a dirtier rag. The air was thick with tobacco smoke and the smell of cheap whiskey.

When we came through the door all conversation stopped. Chan stepped about six or eight feet to my left and we looked the place over. "There's five Rocking M horses outside," I said. "I figure that means there's five skunks in here."

One of the men playing cards took a cigar from his mouth and looked up. "Who the hell are you?"

"Ben Hawkins. I'm foreman of the Reverse Box E."

"Might be you were. Seems to me there ain't no Reverse Box E no more."

"You ride for the Rocking M?"

"Un-huh. What of it?"

"You got a choice," I said. "You can draw, or leave your guns here and ride out of the country."

One of the other men at the table stood up. "Whoa," he said. "You all hang on a minute. I got no part of this."

He backed away to a far corner. Another man at the table followed him. There was a general rush that way, and when it was over, only the three men at the bar and two at the table remained. The two at the table stood up. "Two against five," the man with the cigar said. "You sure take a lot on yourself."

"Nothing we can't handle. Which will it be, you going to ride or fight?"

Chan spoke then, and his voice was enough to curl paint. "You take those two at the table, Hawkins. These boys at the bar are mine."

"He'p yourself."

For a long minute nobody spoke. Then the man with the cigar puffed hard, took the cigar from his mouth, and laid it down. "Ah, hell," he said. "Why not?"

Then he drew. I'd been holding my Winchester down by my leg, and when he drew I just tilted the barrel up and fired like it was a pistol. The bullet stuck him in the belly, knocking him back and down.

The second man had his Colt out and our shots crossed. His bullet snapped by me, coming too close. My own bullet struck his shoulder, spun him around. I fired again and his mouth erupted blood and broken teeth. He folded up and went down.

Chan's Colt boomed behind me, four shots coming so close together they sounded almost like one. A pause, then he fired a fifth shot. The air was dense with powder smoke and I stepped sideways, trying to see.

The man I'd shot in the stomach was up on his knees. His left hand was clutching at his stomach, but his right hand still held a gun. He tried to bring it in line and I fired again, hitting him in the throat. His eyes went round and his mouth opened wide. Then his eyes rolled back in his head and he fell forward onto his face, his Colt exploding into the floor.

I swung the rifle around toward the bar, but there was

no need. Two of the men there were on the floor, one dead, the other going fast. The third man still stood, but a bullet had shattered his right wrist. Pain was written all over his face and he moaned softly.

Chan was reloading his Colt. When he finished I walked up to the bar. The bartender had dropped down behind the barrels when the shooting started, and he stood up slowly.

"Mister," I said, "I figure you get two kinds of customers here, Rocking M riders and rustlers. You want to stay in business, you tell the Rocking M riders they'd best leave the country.

"And you pass the word that anybody stealing Reverse Box E beef had best look at his hole card. We see anybody pushing our cows we won't ask why. That clear?"

He shrugged. "I'll pass the word. Don't know as they'll listen."

"You show 'em the bloodstains on the floor," I said. "Might be that'll be persuading."

The Rocking M rider with the busted wrist was a younger fellow, likely no more'n twenty. His face was pale and the only thing keeping him on his feet was the bar. He looked at me, and I saw pain mixed with fear in his eyes.

"What about my wrist?" he asked. "What'll I do?"

I sighed. "Lay your hand out there on the bar, and I'll take a look."

Chan's bullet had cut through the wrist, breaking the bone before going its way. The bone looked to be a fairly clean break. Picking up a bottle of whiskey from the bar, I poured it over the wound. He groaned and nearly fell. Using my bandanna, I tied his wrist as best I could.

"That'll hold you until you get to a doctor," I said.

"That's all you're going to do?"

Chan tossed a forty-five cartridge onto the bar. It was dented deeply where the firing pin had struck. "You count yourself lucky it's just your wrist," Chan said. "If that round hadn't been a dud, Hawkins would've had to pour whiskey into your heart. Now you go on out of here and find yourself a sawbones, else I might see how many more dud cartridges I got."

The man turned another shade paler and stumbled outside. A minute or so later we heard the sound of a horse racing away.

"McKay and the others'll be wondering what happened to me," I said. "We'd best get on the trail."

We left that place at a trot, heading west. It was a long ways down to where Beth, McKay, and the others were camped, and all along the trail my mind was going round and round, looking for a way to stop Pierce.

Being late, we pushed hard, and came in sight of the ridge I was looking for just two days later. By then I had an idea forming. It wasn't quite complete, but it was coming along fine.

CHAPTER 22

COME TO FIND OUT, it wasn't only me and Chan who'd been through the mill out there. Fact was, Chan was the only man in camp who wasn't hurt one way or another. McKay had a knife cut in his leg that was wide and deep, Billy had his head wound busted open, Harry had a bullet wound in his side, and Paul had a broken nose.

Harry and Paul had been gone the shortest time, just five days in all. They told their tale first.

"We come on half a dozen Rocking M boys pushing a fair-sized bunch of cattle—five hundred or so, I'd say. Stampeding them looked like an easy job, so we gave it a try.

"We laid up in some rocks with our rifles, and knocked two men from the saddle with our first shots. The cattle started running, and it looked like we'd done fine."

"Looked that way," Paul said. "Would've been fine, too. 'Cept for those other ten men."

"What ten men?" I asked.

"The ten who'd been riding back behind the herd, just waiting for a couple of damn fools to try something," Paul said. "They came charging up and near had us cold. As it was, we had a running battle for two hours."

"We were almost away," Harry said, "only some of those Rocking M fellas knew the country too damned well. Four of them slipped away from the bunch following us and somehow got ahead. We rode right into them.

"I caught a bullet in the side, and it's just damned luck we wasn't both killed."

"How'd you get away?" Chan asked.

Paul shook his head. "Harry rode right off a cliff, and I was dumb enough to follow. That's where I got this busted nose. The horses skidded on their rumps most of the way down, then they lost it and we went head over teakettle.

"Don't see how in the world we weren't both killed. If you'll look back yonder you'll see we both came back on different mounts . . . courtesy of two obliging Rocking M men we came across.

"I swear on my mother's grave, if I ever have to make a choice again betwixt getting shot or going over a cliff, I'll have to give long thought to the bullet."

"Hell," Harry said, "I don't know what you're complaining about. I took a bullet *and* went over the cliff."

I looked to McKay. His leg was bandaged heavily. "Might as well tell us about it," I said.

"Not much to tell. Me and Billy found where Pierce was bunching up a hell of a lot of cattle . . . maybe three thousand or thereabouts. Looks like he's fixing to move them over the Pecos, letting them graze as they go.

"Anyway, they had way the hell too many men around the herd for us to get close, so we rode wide around and went to take a look at Pierce's house.

"He's got that place set up for war. He's built a new bunkhouse on the far side of the house, and between the two they can cover every inch of ground with rifle fire. And he's hired himself an army.

"Best I can tell, Pierce has twenty or thirty men out guarding his cattle, another fifteen or twenty out hunting us at any given time, and at least fifteen right there with him. Likely that's a low count, too. And he keeps that whole place lit up at night. Got lanterns hanging everywhere."

"There's enough to go around," I said. "That don't explain the knife wound."

"Had a run-in with one of the guards. He got a knife in my leg before I could get a bullet in him."

"Guess it's your turn, Billy. How'd you get your head busted open like that?"

Billy looked sour. "I'd just as soon not talk about it."

"Ah, hell, Billy," McKay said. "You might as well tell 'em. It could've happened to anybody."

Billy's voice was a whisper. "Got butted by a goat," he said.

"You what?"

"You heard me," he said. "I got butted by a goat, goldang it. I thought I saw a man squatting in the bushes waiting to jump McKay, so I dived in on him. Turned out it was a damn goat, and he saw me coming quick enough to swing his head around and catch me a good one."

We all laughed. Billy turned red. "It was dark," he said. "And it looked like a man."

"Gives a new meaning to the term Billy goat," Paul said. We laughed harder. Billy reddened all the more.

Me and Chan laid out our story then, keeping it to bare bones. When we finished, McKay shook his head. "I'm sure sorry to hear about Travis and Tom. But I'm damn glad you got a bullet in Campbell. I hope it festers up and kills him slow.

"While we're on the subject of Campbell, I got some bad news. Beth, you recall Charly Ford?"

"Of course. He only runs about a hundred head of cattle, but he's always talking about becoming a big rancher."

"Brice Campbell killed him," McKay said. "Shot him dead right in front of his wife. He did that and threatened the other small ranchers. Told them to pack up and get out, and mostly they did.

"The ones that stayed are lying low, waiting to see who wins. We won't get no help from them."

Beth's eyes filled with tears. Her voice was broken when she spoke. "There's been so many men killed," she said. "It isn't worth all this killing. Maybe we should ride away and let Pierce have the land."

"I reckon that's up to you," I said. "You're paying the wages."

"But you don't want to ride away, do you?"

"Beth, it's like I said, you pay the wages, and I can't speak for the others, noway. Only, Pierce has taken things too far. Just like you said, too many men have already died, and a lot of them have been ours. It's personal now, and I got to see it through."

She nodded slowly.

"What'll we do next?" McKay asked. "We keep going at Pierce like this he'll whittle us down one by one."

"Next we rest for a week or two," I said. "We rest, we eat, and we heal. Then we hit Pierce right where he lives."

"Hell," McKay said, "we wouldn't stand a chance. I told you, he's got fifteen or twenty men there all the time. And he knows damn well we ain't got but six or eight."

"I think I know where we can get help," I said. "If it works out we'll stand a chance."

"Where you going to find help out here?" Billy asked. "There ain't nothing for miles about but rattlesnakes and rustlers."

"I'll tell you later," I said. "I still have some thinking to do. Right now I want to eat, shave, and sleep for three days."

That's pretty much what I did. Scraping that beard off my face felt so good that I went ahead and took the mustache off with it. Then I ate till I was fit to burst, and slept a solid ten hours. It was in my mind that some of the boys would rib me about sleeping so long, and they might've . . . had they not been sleeping themselves.

Along about the fourth day I was sitting down by the water hole, smoking and thinking. Beth walked over and sat down close by. For a time she just looked at me.

"Ben," she said at last, "have you given any thought to what you'll do when this is over? If we win, I mean."

"Not much. I'd like to have my own smithy. Maybe start

a livery and catch a few wild mustangs to sell. Might even buy a few acres of land.

"I'm not looking for nothing fancy, nor to get rich. But I don't know how many good years I got left in me, Beth. If I can make wages without working for another man, I'll be more'n satisfied."

She drew her knees up to her chin. "Have you thought about staying here? I'll need help rebuilding the ranch. And . . . oh, hell, Ben. I've been a widow for too long. . . . I like you, Ben, and I'd like to have you there with me. I guess that's as plain as I can say it."

It was like the air went right out of me. I sat there, not knowing what to say.

"You do like me, don't you, Ben?"

I rolled a cigarette, lit it. "Beth, you're a fine, lovely woman. Strong willed, independent, and a lady. I can't imagine a man not liking you. Only, well, I reckon you caught me off guard. I don't know what to say."

She touched my cheek, looked into my eyes. "Maybe this is the wrong time to talk about it, but give it some thought, Ben. Promise me that much?"

"I'll sure think about it," I said.

Beth walked back up to the camp, leaving me feeling like I'd been hit between the eyes with a whiffletree. I'd never had truck with any proper woman, except to tip my hat and say hello. Women like Ruby had always been my style. I'd never even had a courting girl, even as a lad, and the possibility of marriage never even came up.

Not that I hadn't thought about it. When a man's out riding the free, far range alone, there ain't much to do but think. And when you're riding into the teeth of a cold north wind, your hat held on and your ears kept warm by an old bandanna tied over your head and under your jaw, those thoughts can get wild.

But foolish daydreams meant only to pass the time was

the closest I'd ever come to hitching up. It made a man think. It surely made a man think.

After a bit I walked back up to camp. Chan had gone out earlier, looking for fresh meat, and he was coming back up the trail. He rode into camp with forty pounds of good beef over his saddle.

"It's Rocking M beef," he said. "If Pierce is going to shoot us all, least he can do is feed us first. I'll ride out and get the rest later. Best get to it before the coyotes do."

That's pretty much the way it went for ten days. On the morning of the eleventh day, I figured we'd rested long enough. None of us were healed proper, but we couldn't wait. I knew what I wanted to do and how to go about it.

"McKay," I said, "you and Harry still need some time to heal, but time's a-wasting. I figure you can stay here and rest a bit more, keep an eye on Beth."

"What'll the rest of you do?"

"Hunt some rustlers," I said. "Jim Macklin and his bunch, to be exact."

"They need shooting, right enough," McKay said. "But why now?"

"Don't figure to shoot them," I said. "I figure to hire them on."

McKay jumped. "Hire them on? Are you loco?"

"Probably. Only, I got an idea. Way things are now, they can pick out forty or fifty head now and then, but they got to sell them in Mexico, and they'll be lucky to make drinking money once it's split up.

"Anyway, I got an idea they might go for. Might be they won't, but it's the best chance I see."

"They'll probably shoot you on sight," McKay said. "You ask me, you're barking up the wrong tree. Macklin don't give a damn about nothing except quick money, and lots of it."

"That's what I'm counting on. If he thought any other way I wouldn't try him."

"When will you leave?"

"Soon as we can pack. I figure me, Chan, Paul, and Billy. How about it, Billy? You up to a hard ride on a fool's errand?"

Billy had been spending most of the ten days whittling himself a new wooden leg. He'd finished hollowing out a space at the top for his stub and tacking in a lining. Now he was quickly shaping the bottom.

"You know it," he said.

The four of us were saddled and ready to ride not long after noon. Billy had his new leg in place, and it fit the stirrup better than the old one had.

"How long will you be?" McKay asked.

"No telling. Best count on eight or ten days anyway. Might be shorter or longer, but if we ain't back in two weeks, you can start worrying."

"You ain't back in two weeks," he said, "I'll start hunting."

Beth walked over to me, took hold of my vest. "You be careful, Ben Hawkins."

"Yes, ma'am. I usually am."

She kissed me on the cheek and turned away. I climbed in the saddle and the four of us went looking for Rio Grande Jim.

"Where do you figure to start looking?" Chan asked. "By now Macklin could be anywhere."

"He'll be around," I said. "That little saloon where we shot it out with the Rocking M riders is as good a place as any to start."

"What makes you think he'll be there?"

"Like you said, that's mostly a place for rustlers to stop for a drink on their way to the border and back. If Macklin ain't there now, he'll show sooner or later."

"That bartender could probably tell us right where he is, if he wanted to."

"If he knows," I said, "he'll tell us. He might need a little prodding, but he'll tell us."

Our eyes on the skyline and our hands near our guns, we rode north, looking for a cow thief who had every reason in the world to want me dead.

CHAPTER 23

THIS TIME THERE were no Rocking M horses tied in front of the saloon. Unlike me, Chan hadn't expected to find any. "I doubt Pierce even knows this place exists. If he did, he'd send in a bunch of men and tear it to the ground.

"No," Chan continued, "I think those Rocking M men were playing both sides against the middle. Pierce paid them wages on the one side, and the rustlers paid them for information on the other."

I smiled. "You talk like a man who knows the rustler business."

"Man's got to make a living."

I went through the door first. The bartender gave me the once-over, turned his eyes away. Without the beard and mustache, he plain didn't know me. Then Chan stepped through. Now Chan's got a face a man don't soon forget. The bartender knew him at once. His head swiveled left and right, as though looking for a hole to dive into. There wasn't one.

The saloon was empty except for the bartender and a couple of old Mexicans drinking tequila and playing checkers. We walked up to the bar. That bartender was breaking out in a sweat.

"You got a name?" I asked.

"Sure . . . sure I got a name. It's Logan. Logan Basett."

"Well, Logan, suppose you pour us all a shot of whiskey. Pour one for yourself, too. Looks like you need it."

His hands were shaking as he poured the drinks. He poured one for himself like I'd suggested, threw it down, poured another. "Now that we're drinking buddies," I said, "might be you can help us out."

"Huh? Help you how?"

"Tell us how to find Jim Macklin."

He dropped his glass, spraying the bar with whiskey. He backed away half a step, about all the room he had behind the bar, and brought his hand up in protest. "Mister, you don't know what you're askin'. Macklin ain't nobody to fool with. He'd skin my hide off and hang it out to dry.

"Besides, I don't know where he is. You gotta believe me, I don't know."

Chan moved like a cat, reaching across the bar and grabbing Logan by the hair. He jerked hard, bringing the side of his head down onto the bar. Holding the head down with his left hand, Chan pulled his Colt, stuck the big muzzle right between Logan's eyes.

The sound of the hammer being cocked was loud in the saloon. The old men playing checkers took one look, folded up their checkerboard, and scampered outside. You ain't likely to get as old as they were without knowing when it's time to pack up and go home. Those old men knew.

Logan Basett was almost whimpering in protest. Chan was calm as an August lake. "I'm low on patience," he said, "so I'm only going to ask once. Where can we find Macklin?"

Only a fool could look at Chan and not think he'd pull that trigger. Suddenly Logan Basset was in the mood to talk. "He . . . he came in not long before you were here that last time. Said he was driving a few cattle over the border."

"Hell, we knew that much," Chan said. "You'd better know something we don't."

"He said he'd stop in on his way back. Should be anytime now. There's a little señorita lives in that adobe over yonder there. Macklin favors her. Please, that's all I know. I swear it."

Chan let him up, holstered his Colt. "I 'spect he's telling the truth."

"So do I. Guess we'll wait around a day or two. I'll take the horses out where they can't be seen right off."

Going outside, I led the horses back through the brush, thinking to tie them. Only, in leading them back there, I happened to look behind one of those adobe houses and saw a fine corral.

A burly Mexican was tying a fresh pole onto the corral, and taking a chance, I led the horses over to him. He turned and saw me, stopped what he was doing. First thing I noticed was a big Colt stuck down behind his waistband.

"Buenos días, señor," he said.

"Buenos días. Do you speak American?"

"Sí, a little. Enough."

"We may be here a day or two," I said, "and I saw your corral."

"You wish me to keep your horses?"

"If you can. We'll be glad to pay. Ain't asking nothing for free."

"I sometimes keep horses," he said. "There is grain, and I can cut them grass."

"How much?"

"Two dollars a day, señor. It is little enough."

I grinned. "All right. Keep their saddles handy, though. Might be we'll want to leave in a hurry."

"Sí, I know how it is. They will be ready when you want them."

Going back inside the saloon, I found the others sitting at a table, drinking whiskey and talking. I joined them, poured a shot.

"How long will we wait?" Chan asked.

"Looks like our best chance to find Macklin is right here," I said. "Guess we should give it a week, anyway."

"Hey, barkeep," Paul yelled. "You got anything in the way of food?"

"Beef and beans," Basett said. "There's a Mex woman over yonder that'll give you better."

"How's that?"

"Makes her living cooking for the men who come through. Go careful with her. She don't take no guff."

"I'm hungry, too," I said. "Want to give her a try?"

"Why not?" Billy said. "Can't be any worse than eating our own cooking."

Basett pointed out the adobe. We started out, but Chan turned back and gave Basett a hard look. "Don't get any ideas about leaving," he said. "You do and I'll come find you. My word on it."

"No, sir. I ain't going nowhere."

"You're a good man," Chan said.

It was Billy who knocked on the door of the adobe. When the door opened, a woman of thirty or so stood there. She wore a plain, blue dress and an apron. And she was pretty. The shotgun in her hands wasn't. It was pointed at Billy, but my own gut tightened. One look at her was enough to know she wasn't afraid to use it.

"What do you want?" she asked.

Billy yanked his hat from his head. "The bartender over there said you cooked for folks. We're real hungry, ma'am. And we been eating trail food for a long spell."

"Can you pay?"

"Yes, ma'am," Billy said. "Whatever you ask."

She looked at each of us, then lowered the gun. "Then you may come in. My name is Marcella Diaz."

We went inside. The main room of the adobe was set up with a long table. A deacon's bench sat against a far wall, a comfortable-looking chair near it. Next to the chair was a lamp and a pile of books. A painting of desert mountains hung on the wall nearest the chair.

There was nothing fancy about the place, but it was clean and fine looking.

"Sit down," she said. "I will bring food when it is ready."

It didn't take all that long. She brought out a pot of coffee and four cups first, then a platter of beef and a bowl of corn fixed Mexican style, mixed with red and green peppers. Then she carried out a big loaf of bread and fresh butter, and topped that with frijoles.

It'd been a coon's age since any of us had eaten as well, and we did justice to the food. We finally leaned back in our chairs, full and happy. "How much do we owe you?" I asked.

"Three American dollars," she said. "The food is hard to get out here."

Chan pulled a five-dollar gold piece from his pocket, tossed it to Marcella. "That should cover it," he said.

"I sell only food, señor. This is too much."

"No, ma'am," Chan said. "When you been eating trail food for weeks on end like we been doing, it ain't too much at all."

We went back over to the saloon. Twice during the walk I noticed Chan glancing back toward Marcella Diaz's adobe.

"She was a fetching woman," I said.

"You know it. Always admired a woman with fire."

Four days passed, and we were all getting on edge. All except for Chan, maybe. He never seemed flustered about nothing. And he'd been spending almost as much time over at Marcella's as at the saloon. It didn't seem likely he was spending all that time putting away food, but he offered no explanation and we didn't ask.

Late on the fifth day we were drinking hot beer, talking about how much longer to wait. Then Billy walked over to the window and looked out. "Riders coming in from the west," he said. "At least a dozen. Maybe more."

"All right," I said. "Grab yourselves a corner. Trouble starts, tip a table over and duck down behind it."

Chan took a quick look out a window. "Won't help much," he said. "I count fifteen men out there."

We took our places and waited. They reached the saloon five minutes later, then took a minute or two getting their horses tied. When they came in, it was quick, Rio Grande Jim leading the way. Some spread out along the bar, others sat down at empty tables.

They noticed us right off, but didn't seem bothered by four men. I had my hat pulled low and my head tipped down a bit so my face didn't show. All I could see of Macklin was his boots.

With fifteen of them and only four of us, they didn't much give a damn who we were. But with us sitting around in the corners like we were, it came to Macklin at last that maybe he ought to be curious about us. He walked a bit closer to my table. "You," he said. "Who the hell are you?"

Tipping my hat back, I looked up. " 'Lo, Macklin."

He jumped like he'd stepped on a snake. "Hawkins! Well, I'll be a son of a bitch. You got more guts than a man could fit in a washtub. How'd you find this place?"

"It wasn't all that hard."

"You're shot with luck, Hawkins. Most times there's four or five Rocking M riders here."

"Not anymore. Me and Chan over there paid a visit here couple of weeks back."

"Just the two of you? What happened to the Rocking M men?"

"There was five here when we came in. We sent one of them riding out with a bullet through his wrist."

"The other four?"

I shrugged. "They were bleeding on the floor when we left. I 'spect they're buried somewheres about. You'll have to ask ol' Logan there."

One of Macklin's men pushed through the crowd and came over to the table. "I figured we'd meet again," he said. "Now, by God, we got you. I'm going to take pleasure in killing you."

"Stu—that's your name, ain't it?"

"That's right."

"Well, Stu, suppose you go over there and sit down like a good boy so I don't have to spank you again."

"*What?* Well, damn you to hell!"

His hand dropped for his gun, but Macklin stopped him. "Not now. I'll say when and if."

"But—"

"You questioning me, Stu?"

"No, but that damned—"

"Then do like I say. Get over there with the others."

Stu backed away reluctantly, but he went. Macklin walked over to the bar, came back with a bottle and two glasses. He sat down, filled a glass, and slid it over to me.

"You got me curious, Hawkins. Why are you here?"

"Came looking for you."

"With four men. You may be long on guts, but you're short on brains. Ain't a man among us don't know how to handle a gun, and handle it well.

"And Stu there's got a point. You near knocked his head off with that shotgun butt. And you know damned well we been running off Reverse Box E beef. Might be we should kill you now. Put ourselves ahead of the game."

"Might put some of you ahead. It don't seem likely the four of us could stop you, but we wouldn't die alone."

"No, that much I'll give you. But that don't mean a thing, and you know it, Hawkins. You best spell out what you want. Then we'll talk . . . or start shooting."

I tossed off the shot of whiskey, gritted my teeth against the burn. "We're going to hit Neal Pierce," I said. "We're going to ride right down his throat and stomp on his gizzard. I want you and your boys on our side.

Macklin's face opened in surprise. Then he laughed, long and hard. When he could speak again, there was still a laugh hiding behind his lips. "Damn, Hawkins, you must be cut from seasoned hickory. There ain't no give in you at all. Hit Pierce? Man, I seen that place. A hundred men couldn't take that ranch."

"A hundred men couldn't take the place," I said, "but twenty men might. Especially if they were pushing a thousand head of stampeding cattle right about four in the morning."

I could see Macklin think about it. "It wouldn't work," he said. "You could get in there, all right, but Pierce has a bunkhouse on either side of his house, and ten riflemen in each.

"Might be they couldn't do us much harm in all the dust and such, but we couldn't hurt them, neither. We'd get shot up for nothing."

"Don't plan to worry about the bunkhouses," I said. "Pierce may have a lot of men out there, but I doubt he has more than one or two in the main house. In all the dust and confusion, I figure to get in there. Neal Pierce is the Rocking M. If I can get to him, the war's over."

Macklin took a shot of whiskey, rolled a smoke. "It might work," he said. "Don't know as I'd bet money on it, but it might work. Pierce sure as hell won't be looking for one man to reach the house and bust in.

"Thing is, even if we went along, what's in it for us? With you two fighting a war, the range is easy pickings."

"Sure it is. But what's it got you? You gather up forty or fifty head, drive over to Mexico, sell 'em cheap. Hell, I'll bet you don't get ten dollars a head for the best of 'em."

"It's still easy money."

"Is it? By the time you split it up, and figure in all the time you spend driving them, I'll bet you ain't making much better than wages. Somebody's going to win this war, Macklin. If Pierce wins, the first thing he'll do is start on the rustlers. And he's got enough men to make it real hot out there."

"And if your side wins?"

"If we win, Pierce will be dead. There'll be five or six thousand head of Rocking M cattle running free, and we won't give a damn who takes 'em. You could slap new brands on every head, run 'em up the trail to market and sell legal. Wouldn't nobody say a word."

Macklin sat quiet for a time. "I got to think on it," he said, "talk it over with the boys. You know the Diaz woman over yonder?"

"Been eating there."

"Why don't you all go over there and get a bite now. I'll come over once I know. It might be tough controlling the boys if they're against it, though."

"Don't worry," I said. "We'll give you a head start out of here."

Macklin smiled. "Hickory," he said. "Pure hickory."

We went on over to Marcella Diaz's. She trotted out coffee, biscuits, fried chicken, and gravy. We'd been there near an hour when Macklin came through the door. He sat down, asked for a cup, and poured himself coffee when Marcella brought it.

"Looks like you found yourself some men," he said. "Couple of things, though."

"Such as?"

"We'll do what we have to, push the cattle, keep a cover fire going, things like that. But we figure anybody crossing that open space up to the house is asking for trouble.

"We'll do our best to keep fire on the bunkhouses, but crossing that open space is still going to be a ride into hell. None of my boys are going through there, and that's final."

"Fair enough. What else?"

"If Campbell's there, and it works out right, he's mine."

"Suits me, but why? You got a personal grudge against Brice Campbell?"

"You might say that. He hung two of my men six or eight weeks back."

"Seems to me hanging's kind of an occupational hazard for a rustler."

Macklin gave me a hard look. "It was *how* he hung 'em that bothered me."

"Huh, how did he hang them?"

"Head down over a slow fire. I can't think of a worse way to die."

CHAPTER 24

IT WAS WORTH the trouble we'd gone through just to see McKay's face when we came riding into camp with Jim Macklin and fourteen of his men following. I can't say McKay, or Beth, for that matter, looked very happy about it. Once I'd gone over things, though, they went along.

Soon as we'd eaten, we had us a war council. The plan was simple enough on the surface, but that didn't mean it would be easy.

"First thing we have to do is round up a thousand head of cattle without Pierce knowing about it," I said. "Anybody know how to go about getting his men off the range for a time?"

"Same way me and Tom pulled the Rocking M men out of Comanche Creek," Chan said.

"We can't shoot up the house," Billy said. "That would put more men right where we don't need them."

"The cattle," McKay said. "That big herd he's guarding so well. He's likely moved them before now, but they'll still be together and well guarded. Suppose we find that herd and have three or four men start a ruckus at the right time?"

"That should work," Macklin said. "That herd represents a big part of Pierce's cattle. Me and the boys been looking for a plan to steal it for weeks."

"All we need is two or three riflemen," I said. "They empty their rifles, maybe throw a couple of sticks of dynamite, and Pierce will have to react."

"Getting close enough to scatter that herd will be tough," Billy said.

"We don't need to scatter it, we just need to make Pierce think we're trying to stampede them. That should be enough to get every rider he has over that way."

"Don't suppose he'd send a few of those in the bunkhouses along?" Macklin asked.

"Not likely."

"Didn't think so, but a man can wish."

"All right, where can we gather cattle the quickest?" I asked. "And where can we hold 'em?"

"Hell, boss," McKay said. "You know where to get them as well as I do."

"Along the Pecos."

"Un-huh. There's cattle scattered all over this country, Rocking M and Reverse Box E alike. No matter what spooked them, sooner or later they'll drift to good grass and water. That means along the Pecos."

"Good, now where do we hold them?"

"For how long?" McKay asked.

"Depends how low it takes to bring enough into a herd. If there's as many along the Pecos as I hope, shouldn't be but a day or two."

"Unless Pierce already has men pushing them," Macklin said. "He ain't one to lose a cow, can he help it."

McKay thought a minute. "Best thing we can do is push them northwest, drive them around and behind Pierce. It'll take a little longer, but we won't have to hold the herd anywhere."

"We got to go look," Macklin said. "We need to get in the saddle and look the country over. It's the only way to know where the cattle are, and to plan proper."

I nodded. "McKay, Harry, you two able to ride hard?"

"We been ready for a week," McKay said.

"Great," Beth said. "That means I'll be out here by myself again."

Chan shook his head. "I don't think so. We been coming

and going from here too much. And this time we got better'n twenty men leaving a trail.

"Nope, any of Pierce's men come across a trail that big
leading off into this wilderness, they'll follow it sure."

"You have a better idea?" I asked.

"Fact is, I do. Marcella Diaz. We can put Mrs. Alison up
right there."

"We left tracks over that way too."

"Sure, but that's cattle country. A body expects to find
trails through there. Can't think of a place where she'll
be safer."

"He has a point," Macklin said. "And sure as hell nobody
will search Marcella's place without her permission. That
shotgun of hers argues her point real well."

"Think she'll do it?"

"Know she will," Chan said. "Slip her a few dollars, but
she'll do it."

That's how we went about it. Three days later Beth was
tucked in with Marcella Diaz . . . she'd asked for fifty dollars to put Beth up. Beth agreed, promising a nice bonus
if things worked out.

The rest of us rode wide around Rocking M range, came
in on the Pecos about seventy miles southwest, started
working our way back. Right off, we got lucky. We found
half a dozen Rocking M hands already doing what we
wanted, gathering cattle and easing them back toward
Rocking M range.

They had six hundred or so, with more coming in all
the time. Now and then a new Rocking M rider would
come along, but at no time did they have more than ten
men in camp. Usually it was eight or less.

"That's our ticket," Macklin said. "We wait until they get
enough in a bunch, then we take 'em. Hell, they'll have a
thousand head pulled together in another day or two."

"How do we take the herd?" I asked.

Macklin didn't smile. "The last thing in the world they'll

be expecting is twenty men. We wait for night, take out the guards, then ride right into their camp. Trust me, Hawkins. Stealing cattle is what we do for a living. I know how to take a herd."

We lay back in the hills for two days. Whatever else the Rocking M men were, they were fine cowboys. Cattle came to the Pecos for water, and more than a few were picked up just by driving the herd along, but they went out and pulled in plenty, too.

By the morning of the third day they had the thousand head we wanted. "Tonight," Macklin said. "We take the herd tonight."

We'd had scouts out looking for Pierce's main herd, and they'd found it across the Pecos, right where McKay figured it would be. It meant we couldn't cross the Pecos and drive wide around that way for fear of running into some of the men guarding that herd, and there were plenty.

We pondered it a spell. There seemed only one way left. "Straight in," I said. "We take that herd tonight, and take it straight in.

"We're just about a day's drive from the ranch if we push them hard, and that should work out about right."

"That won't give us time to hit the main herd and pull Pierce's men off the range," Macklin said. "We run into a big bunch of them along the drive, it'll all go for nothing."

Harry ground out his cigarette. "Now that ain't necessarily so," he said. "You remember what me and Paul ran into?"

It took a minute, but I understood. "You mean pull the same stunt? We push the herd with six or seven men, about what Pierce thinks we got, and have the others ride back a piece?"

"That's the ticket," Harry said. "Anybody sees the dust we raise and comes looking, we'll have a nasty surprise waiting."

"Bueno. Macklin, once we take the herd, you and your

men can ride back a quarter mile or so. Any of Pierce's men hits us, you should be able to hit back hard."

"All right. First we got to take the herd, though. Now's the time to catch some shut-eye. It's going to be a busy night."

Most of us managed a few winks of sleep through the day, but it was tough. We were backed off from the herd far enough to risk a small fire, so we made coffee. Fact is, we made coffee half a dozen times. And we drank it all.

The moon was a yellow sliver in a starry sky . . . just right for stealing cattle, or so Macklin told me. There were two night riders out with the herd, and taking them was surprisingly easy. Macklin simply sent a man riding up to each of them, making no effort to keep quiet. Macklin said those night riders would think it was somebody from their own camp coming out, and they did.

Right when Macklin's men were nearing the night riders, the rest of us stuck spurs to our horses and hit the camp full tilt, pistols out. They heard us coming quick enough to grab weapons, then we were on them. All four men in camp were shot to ribbons in seconds.

I didn't hear the two shots from out near the herd that killed the night riders, but minutes later Macklin's men came riding in. "Best get some men out there with the cattle," one of them said. "Those shots spooked them."

Half a dozen of us went out. Harry and McKay hauled off the bodies of the night riders from the herd while the rest of us sang and brought the cattle back under control. McKay rode up to me, spoke low.

"Boss, I know this is war, but I can't say I liked what happened here tonight. Those men weren't gunfighters. Cowboys, that's what they were. Plain damn-fool cowboys, and they never had a chance."

"Can't say I like it, either. I keep telling myself this'll be the end of it, but I don't like it."

We all took turns sleeping in snatches that night, half a

dozen men on guard at all times. Come morning we started the herd northwest, staying south of the river, heading straight toward Neal Pierce's house. I can't say how the others felt, but my gut was tied in knots, expecting a bunch of Pierce's men to show up on the skyline at any moment.

It wasn't like Brice Campbell. He was supposed to be one of the best at what he did, but the only groups out hunting us lately had been fairly easy to elude. Was he losing his touch? Or hell, maybe his reputation was overblown?

When we did see Rocking M riders, it wasn't quite as expected. Along about four in the afternoon, three men showed on the skyline, rode a bit closer, suddenly reined in. One of them upped with a rifle and fired a shot. It knocked a cow down. Then the three men turned and stuck spurs to their horses.

Macklin saw it all, and he came running. Macklin and most of his men rode to the herd, but four others took off after the Rocking M riders.

"If they get away," I said, "Pierce will have an army waiting for us."

"They ain't going nowhere," Macklin said. "They won't get two miles."

He was right. A bit later his men came back, one of them with a wicked bullet wound in his foot. "Son of a buck turned in the saddle and snapped off a shot from three hundred yards," he said. "Don't know if he was lucky or good, but he sure caught my foot a good one."

Macklin pulled off the man's boot. "You lost a toe. Can you ride?"

"Hell, yes, I can ride. Let me get a bandage slapped on it, and I'll be right with you. Funny, but it don't hurt none at all."

"Not yet," Macklin said, "but it will. We got to cauterize it."

"Aw, hell, ain't there no other way?"

"Nope. Won't take long."

Macklin built a small fire, laid the blade of his knife in the coals. When the steel of the knife blade was glowing red, he removed it. "You ready, hoss?"

Sweat glistened on the man's head. "Get on with 'er."

Macklin wrapped his arm around the ankle to keep the foot steady, pressed the glowing blade against the open wound. Steam and the smell of burning flesh rose into the air. The man screamed through gritted teeth.

"It'll heal fine now," Macklin said. "Still think you can ride?"

"I can ride."

Pushing cattle after dark is a tricky thing. You have to know the land, and you have to know cattle. But when dark came, we kept pushing. It was midnight or so when we came into long sight of the Pierce house. It was lit up like high noon.

I'd fused and capped the dynamite earlier. Now I passed it out to Macklin's men. "Don't take no chances," I said, "but if you get close enough, that might rattle those men in the bunkhouses.

"Cut left and right and get clear before those riflemen can get you in a crossfire. Just give me enough cover to reach the house."

"For us to reach the house," Macklin said. "I'm going in with you."

"You? I thought none of you were willing to take that kind of chance?"

"I said none of my men would. Didn't say nothing about myself."

"You want Brice Campbell that bad?"

"That's right, I want Brice Campbell that bad."

"Welcome to him," I said. "You ready?"

"Ready as I'll ever be."

Pulling my rifle from the scabbard, I pointed it in the air. "All right," I yelled, "get 'em running."

I fired my rifle and yelled for all I was worth. Twenty other gunshots shattered the night, and the cattle broke into a run.

Mister, if you've never seen a thousand head of cattle break into a dead run in the middle of the night, you've missed a sight. The ground rumbled and shook, and the air was filled with dust and dirt and the bawling of cattle. Four of Macklin's men were riding swing and point, trying to keep the cattle headed toward the ranch house.

One thing I learned right then . . . rustlers know as much about moving cattle as any cowboy, and more than most. I guess stealing cattle by night gives you a kind of experience you can't get no other way.

Kicking my horse hard, I forced him right into the mass of cattle, praying he wouldn't stumble. If he went down I wouldn't live long enough to know what happened.

Macklin was close by, fighting to keep his own horse up. I couldn't worry about him or anything else. Ahead of us I saw a man run from one of the bunkhouses, shouting. He raised his rifle and fired.

Then we were into the ranch yard itself. It sounded like a thousand guns hammering out shots. A bullet clipped through the mane of my claybank, another tore the hat from my head. Then a stick of dynamite exploded, followed quickly by another. For a few seconds the shooting from the bunkhouses stopped. It was just long enough.

The house was right there in front of me and I left the saddle at a dive. Something moved in the corner of my eye. Turning my head, I saw Johnny standing on the porch, a Colt in his hand. This time he didn't hesitate. He fired just as I dived headfirst for a window.

Something struck me hard in the side, then I was crashing through. I hit the floor, came up to one knee. A man loomed in front of me and I fired. He went down and I fired a second time. Shots rang out close by, then Macklin came through the door shoulder first.

A long staircase ran up the left wall, and from somewhere above I heard Pierce's voice ring out. "Who's down there? What the hell is going on?"

A shot came through from another room, smacking into the wall right behind me. I rolled away and Macklin fired. The staircase was right there. It had quieted down outside, the stampeding cattle fading off into the distance. We didn't have much time.

"Go," Macklin yelled. "I'll keep them busy down here."

Taking a deep breath, I charged up the staircase, not knowing what to expect. A man suddenly stepped in front of me. I jammed the rifle barrel into his stomach and fired. He screamed and fell forward, hands grasping for a hold. He caught my rifle, pulling it from my hands as he fell past me down the stairs.

Pulling my Colt, I thumbed back the hammer and ran up to the landing, turning down a hallway without hesitating. Pierce was right there in front of me, a double-barreled shotgun in his hands. I threw myself against the wall as he fired. The roar was deafening, and pellets tore at my left arm.

Pierce had pulled both triggers; if he hadn't, I'd have been dead. The shotgun was already opened, and he was trying to shove shells into the chambers. I aimed, fired. The bullet struck Pierce in the chest, knocking him backward. I fired twice more and he went down, the shotgun flying from his hands.

He slid down the wall into a sitting position. "Knew . . . I should . . . have hired you on . . . Hawkins."

Cocked pistol still in my hand, I walked over and knelt down in front of him, opened his shirt. All three bullets had hit where they mattered. "There ain't nothing I can do," I said.

Blood trickled from the corner of his mouth. "Should . . . should have listened . . . to you. Should have taken that offer. I just . . . wanted it all."

His head rolled to the side and he died. The shooting outside had stopped, though two shots rang out from downstairs. I yelled down. "Macklin, tell 'em it's over. Pierce is dead."

Looking out a window, I saw men coming from the bunkhouses, moving toward the house. Sliding open the window, I put a bullet at a man's feet. "There's nothing left to fight for," I yelled. "Your boss is dead."

"You're alive," one of them yelled. "That's reason enough to keep shooting."

"Mister, we got thirty men out there with dynamite. You willing to die for a man who's already dead?"

Now, that was a bluff, and might be they knew it. But they'd seen the last of their wages. That, and Johnny Stevens, made the difference. I heard him yell out from somewhere downstairs. His words were faint, but I understood them.

"Let me go out and talk to them," he yelled.

"Go ahead," Macklin yelled back. "Just be careful how you go about it."

A minute later I saw Johnny stride into the yard. By the light from the lanterns, I could tell his shirt was stained with blood. "He's right," Johnny said. "The war's over."

"Over, hell," a man said. "He killed the boss."

"That's the point," Johnny said. "I rode for the brand just like you, but the brand is dead. There ain't no need for nobody else to die. Hawkins, you can come on out. Won't nobody shoot."

I started down the hallway. A voice from one of the rooms stopped me. It sounded almighty weak. "Hawkins, is that you out there?"

Thumbing back the hammer on my Colt, I slowly pushed open the door to the room. A bed was right in my line of sight, and in the bed was Brice Campbell. He looked like a shell of his old self.

"Hello, Hawkins."

"Hello, Brice. My bullet do that?"

"Hell, yes. Still don't know how you got in range so damned fast."

"Luck, mostly. Lucky a lot of ways, I reckon. I wondered how we made it so far. Now I know."

Brice tried to sit up straighter, failed. "I'll take that as a compliment," he said.

"It was meant as one. You going to live?"

"Doc said he figured I would. Don't know as I want to, though. Can't move my legs much. Sure as hell can't walk.

"They tell me the feeling might come back . . . or I might be in a wheelchair the rest of my life."

"That's tough, Brice."

Macklin came through the door, saw Campbell, and raised his Colt. "Go ahead," Brice said. "I'd take it as a favor."

For long seconds I could see Macklin trying to decide. Then he eased down the hammer and holstered the Colt. "Doing you a favor is the last thing in the world I'd do," he said. He turned and walked from the room.

My head was spinning, and my side hurt something fierce. Getting back down the stairs was a hell of a lot tougher than getting up had been. Macklin's men must have been watching from out yonder, because by the time I reached the porch they were there. Nobody tried to stop them.

Johnny came over and sat down on the porch beside me. His left arm was limp, and blood ran from a bullet cut on his neck. He looked at me. "Who won, Ben? You tell me. Who the hell won?"

I shook my head. "Nobody won, Johnny. Nobody ever does."

CHAPTER 25

ONE THING ABOUT Beth Alison—she wasn't a woman to waste time. Two weeks after Pierce's death she was already trying to put her own ranch back together. She had enough money to pay us off and to hire a bunch of cowhands to scour the range for Reverse Box E cattle.

The bank in Austin gave her enough of a loan to get started on rebuilding the house, with Beth using the cattle as collateral. She'd be fine if she could get the herd to market in one piece, though even then it'd take five or six years to build back up to where she was before the war started.

She'd used near the last of her cash money to order more barbed wire, and I reckon she couldn't be blamed. With the Rocking M out of the picture, a lot of small ranchers were going to come running into the hole Pierce left.

Macklin was busy, too. Him and his men were rounding up Rocking M cattle day and night. He came over to the saloon once and we talked for a time.

"Registered me a brand," he said. "The Circle M."

I had to smile. "Let me guess, your branding iron ain't nothing but a circle?"

"You know it. All it does is stretch the rocker on the Rocking M brand all the way around."

He had two shots of whiskey and a plate of food, then stood up. "Got to be getting back," he said. "Everybody and their grandmas are grabbing Rocking M cattle. And rustlers are thick as fleas on a hound.

"Hell of a note, ain't it? Couple of weeks back I was stealing cattle, and now I'm trying to keep mine from being stole. Hell of a world. Be seeing you, Hawkins."

Billy was hanging about town, but neither of us had seen Johnny. Chan Fowler came through, driving a by-God buggy, Marcella Diaz beside him. He stopped in to say goodbye. "Fellow I rode with a couple of years back came from Oregon," he said. "Way he described it made it sound real pretty. We're going to try our hand there."

Seemed like I was the only one not busy. The wound in my side wasn't too serious, but it'd torn some muscle. Doc said I shouldn't ride a horse for at least a month, else I'd rip it wide open.

I had other hurts as well, and the truth was I needed a month to hole up in more ways than one. Red Heinlin let me stay in my old room, even though he knew I couldn't work at the smithy.

Beth came by now and again. She spoke of the house going up like it was ours. For a while there I didn't know how I felt, nor what I wanted to do. Then came a day when me and Beth were talking, and a wagon loaded to over-flowing with rolls of barbed wire came through. I watched it go by, and Beth read my face. Her shoulders sank.

"You aren't going to stay, are you, Ben?"

I looked at her. "Ah, hell, Beth. I like you. I like you fine. It's only, hell, I don't know. This ain't what I want, is all."

"Where will you go?"

I shrugged. "I told Johnny once that barbed wire was the coming thing, and there was no stopping it. He told me I couldn't like it. I reckon we was both right.

"I've had my fill of cattle drives, but there's other things to do. Might be I can't stop barbed wire. Hell, I know I can't. But I can follow the wild wind and maybe stay ahead of it for a time. Long enough to see me through."

Beth's face was a blank. She touched my hand. "I think I always knew this is how it would be."

"I'm sorry, Beth. Sorry as anything."

"So am I, Ben."

She turned and left. That was the last time I ever spoke to Beth Alison. That evening I was in the saloon, sitting with Billy, drinking beer and waiting for a seat in a poker game. I told Billy about my plans.

"Where'll you go, Ben?"

"West, I reckon. New Mexico, maybe on to Arizona. Find some little town that needs a good blacksmith. Open a livery on the side, catch some mustangs and sell 'em. Don't know as a man can get rich that way, but it sure beats hob out of punching cattle."

"Don't suppose you could use a partner?"

"Meaning you? Hell, yes. Never did like riding alone."

While we were sitting there, Johnny Stevens walked into the saloon, his arm bandaged and in a sling. His eyes met mine, then he walked toward the bar. I stood up, groaning at the pull in my side. Walking over to Johnny, I leaned on the bar for support.

"I'd buy you a drink," I said, "but I figure you owe me one."

He looked straight at me. "I wasn't sure you'd want anything to do with me," he said.

"Hell, why not? We rode into this country together, didn't we? Seems we ought to ride out the same way. Come on over to the table and we'll tell you about it."

Johnny smiled. The three of us talked things over, then Billy asked where Johnny had been staying.

"Out at the Rocking M," Johnny said. "Or what's left of it. Tending Brice a good bit of the time. He's getting better, but it don't look like he'll ever walk right.

"There's talk that Pierce had some relatives up north, but by the time they find out what's going on it'll be way too late. Another month and there won't be a Rocking M cow left in Texas."

Ruby came down the stairs, swished over beside me. She

sat down, and Billy told her about our plans. "When are you leaving?"

"Soon as I can ride. Couple of weeks, maybe."

"Do you know where you're going?"

"Hell, no. West. There's a little town somewheres over that way that's right. We'll find her."

"Will that town have a saloon?"

"If it don't, we'll keep right on going. Why?"

"I don't think Comanche Creek has much of a future now. Let me know when you get where you're going, Ben. Might be I'll come see you."

"Anytime."

Ruby went over to the bar and started hustling drinks. Standing up, I rolled a cigarette and went out on the boardwalk. Bob Parker had been on my mind. At first it galled me, thinking about him getting away with selling us out. The thought of going after him was strong. Then I thought, *The hell with it.*

Men like Bob Parker are born running toward their death. One of us would come across him sooner or later. Or he'd pull the same kind of trick a second time and not get away with it. Either way, to hell with him.

It was near dark, only the top edge of the sun showing above the horizon. The day had been a hot one, and as it often does, the coolness of sunset brought with it a strong, gusty, wild wind. It was blowing west, toward the last free range.

"Keep right on blowing," I said. "Couple of weeks and we'll be holding your tail and headed west ourselves."

Dropping my cigarette, I ground it out with my heel, then turned and went back inside the saloon.